THE AT-YOUR-BECK
FELICITY CONVEYOR

Reviews

Praise for THE AT-YOUR-BECK FELICITY CONVEYOR: A NOVEL OF SIN & RETRIBUTION (Op. 154)

"This sharply satirical tale exposes the dark side of the American dream and the inevitable consequences of greed."
—NEWINBOOKS.COM

Praise for JAGDLIED: A CHAMBER NOVEL FOR NARRA-TOR, MUSICIANS, PANTOMIMISTS, DANCERS & CULINARY ARTISTS (Op. 20)

"... a literary roller-coaster ... this tour de force is a thriller of linguistic acuity designed to delight a genuine aficionado of the English language ... Love and hate, revenge and redemption, and a diamond-studded thriller atmosphere that demands much from its readers while rewarding its audiences with a compelling, sassy set of characters and conundrums make for a read that is hard to put down ... a story that is especially recommended for literary readers of experimental writings and thrillers which are quite a notch above the standard formula fare."
—DIANE DONOVAN, MIDWEST BOOK REVIEWS

"... unlike anything I have ever read ... you get immersed and entirely consumed by the events ... a roller-coaster that keeps you on the edge of your seat ... the prose was a feast that satiated my mind, eyes, and ears ... an extraordinary reading experience ... Reading this book will

take you on an epic visual-auditory adventure, and is bound to keep you glued to your seat till the very end."
—ONLINE BOOK CLUB

"... monumental ... farcical story ... Perils of Pauline on steroids— modernized, more exaggerated, highly extravagant, and decadent ... lavishly illustrated with drawings that have a sixties Haight- Ashbury summer of love feel to them ... He proves himself a master cartoon- ist that can create a tapestry of masterfully detailed and storytelling images with an astonishing diversity of style and creativity. [Landon's] narrative sweep is so great and so strange that it lends itself readily to graphic depictions and to ... musical accompaniment ... masterful, stylistic and complex. This is a huge book ... uniquely entertaining and truly worth experiencing."
—AUTHORSREADING

"... a thrilling literary ride ... The term 'page turner' was coined for this book ... To the intrigued reader, beware, this book is quite a dirty sex crazed romp. Conservatives better brace themselves, keep a bible handy, and an open mind because you will hate how much you enjoy the erotic quality of this book. Rarely does a book possess so many winning qualities. Humor, drama, erotica, tragedy and much more. All delivered with expert craftsmanship and a generous dose of thrill ... a very enjoyable and entertaining ride."
—LITERARY TITAN (WINNER OF THE LITERARY TITAN BOOK AWARD)

"... a multifaceted novel ... the creative genius of Landon is delivered at full throttle ... I loved this book ... a wholly unique concept ... No scruples, whatsoever. Highly recommended!"
—JAMIE MICHELE, READERS' FAVORITE

"... am flabbergasted ... by the magnitude (bigger than Our Bodies, Ourselves) ... by the multi-media Gesamtkunstwerk ambitions ... by the Joycean wordplay ... exuberant code-switching, diction-mixing, blending of disparate linguistic ingredients into previously unknown harmonies and cacophonies. Like Finnegans Wake or The Anatomy of Melancholy ... I look forward to dipping into it for years to come"

—CHRISTOPHER MILLER (AUTHOR OF "SUDDEN NOISES FROM INANIMATE OBJECTS" & "AMERICAN CORNBALL")

"... creative genius ... unique ... thought-provoking ideas and language ... memorable and enjoyable. I highly recommend this creation as an experience not to be missed!"

—GOLFWELL.NET

"... a work of arts-based literary fiction ... a wild ride ... kept me reading! ... an explosive collection of content ... not for the faint of heart."

—K.C. FINN, READERS' FAVORITE

"... a stunning piece of literature ... took my breath away ... impossible to put down ... unforgettable ... if you are a reader who is tired of reading the same old books that are lackluster and forgettable then take a chance with this one ... you will not be disappointed! This incredible book gets Five Stars from me!"

—AIMEE ANN, RED HEADED BOOKLOVER

"... one of those 'oh my gosh!' books ... entirely colorful and strangely eclectic mix of words ... totally outlandish ... genius ... incredibly complex ... creative ... no denying the cleverness ..."

—ANNE-MARIE REYNOLDS, READERS' FAVORITE

"... Remarkably creative ... simply magnificent ... this is the first 'chamber novel' that I've read ... wonderfully put together. The graphics were vibrant and storytelling ... unique and powerful ... I truly never read anything like it before. The story was filled with satire, darkness and embarked many different aspects about life and human behavior. I enjoyed the entire story and how it all came together, making sense of the wondrous mind of Landon."

—AMY'S BOOKSHELF REVIEWS (listed as the NUMBER ONE BOOK of 2018)

Praise for NOTHING IS MORE: A HIGH BLACK COMEDY IN VERSE WITH MUSIC FOR SIX ACTORS (Op. 92)

"... Shakespearean ... *Nothing is More* ... a satirical black comedy written in doggerel verse. This pun-filled linguistic labyrinth pokes fun at the elitism of the art world and academia while still gracefully tackling large and complex themes in philosophy and aesthetics ... over the top ... a beautifully nuanced unfolding of events ... [Dolly Gray Landon] has an incredible grasp of language and wielded it masterfully, filling the script with deft puns and word mashups ...The juxtaposition of Shakespearean language and blatant, sleazy vulgarity set the stage for clever and entertaining contrasts ... the entire script is a string of twisted-up words, heavy philosophical concepts, and multiple levels of meaning ... I loved this play ... because I am heavily into art history and I enjoy clever wordplay ... [I would] recommend *Nothing is More* to people who have some background in the philosophy of aesthetics and enjoy following numerous metaphysical threads at once."

—ONLINE BOOK CLUB

"... Some of the longer sections of dialogue had much philosophical meat on them and some fascinating insights into the way we view and cherish the opinions of 'artists' and 'experts,' often at the expense of our own common sense or gut feelings ... In many ways I was reminded of a much more extreme FlashHeart from Blackadder, morphing to the extreme pragmatism and cynicism of Blackadder himself ... 'and now for something completely different!'"

—GRANT LEISHMAN, READERS' FAVORITE

"... outrageous. Anyone expecting a staid story or a typical outline of dramatic form is in for both a revelation and a treat ... toss any expectations out the window and settle back for a challenging but unique, rollicking ride as Dolly Gray Landon romps through academia and social inspection with an eye to probing the roots of artistic and social revolution alike ... no group is immune, here. Landon pokes fun at and makes pointed observations of just about everything in this circle, which holds as much potential for offense as it does insight ... a well-crafted, complex, dramatic work that will gain attention not just from innovative drama students and producers, but from readers of plays, who will find it delightfully quirky and whimsical in its creative, complex inspection of the evolution of dogmas and schemes in the art world."

—DIANE DONOVAN, Senior Reviewer of MIDWEST BOOK REVIEWS (July, 2019 edition)

"... an outlandish play ... There is a great deal of poetry in the words Landon delivers in his work ... Landon has penned another enormous and ... complicated theatric treat that once again showcases his brilliance."

—D. HEARNE, AUTHORSREADING

"... a mix between Shakespeare and Joe Dirt ... uniquely written ... hard to put down ... fast pace ... unusual environment ... unique."

—ANTHONY ELMORE, READERS' FAVORITE

"... amusing and engaging right from the start ... entertaining ... exciting ... kept me laughing, entertained, and quickly flipping pages."

—LITERARY TITAN

"... philosophically challenging work ... As many conspire to rebuke ... and uncover the nonsense artist for what he truly is, the schemes take twists and turns to a startling and unusual climax ... Students of both art and philosophy are sure to get a lot out of the ideas discussed by playwright Dolly Gray Landon ... for those who appreciate a critical challenge with plenty of dark laughter, ... sure to bring smirks to lips ... recommended as a powerful intellectual work for a select audience."

—K.C. FINN, READERS' FAVORITE

The At-Your-Beck Felicity Conveyor

A NOVEL OF SIN & RETRIBUTION

DOLLY GRAY LANDON

7TH SPECIES PUBLICATIONS

7TH SPECIES PUBLICATIONS

nolandgary5@gmail.com
website: garynolandcomposer.com

Publisher's Cataloguing-in-Publication Data

Name: Landon, Dolly Gray, author.
Title: The At-Your-Beck Felicity Conveyor: a Novel of Sin & Retribution (Op. 154)
Description: First Edition. | Lake Oswego, OR: Seventh Species Publications, 2025.
Identifiers: ISBN: 979-8-218-46862-0 (pbk.) | 979-8-3302-8828-1 (e-book)
Subjects: Sexual dominance and submission--Fiction. | Man-woman relationships--Fiction | Erotic fiction

"If you forgive the fox for stealing your chickens, he will take your sheep."

—OLD PROVERB

"Scientific fraud, plagiarism, and ghost writing are increasingly being reported in the news media, creating the impression that misconduct has become a widespread and omnipresent evil in scientific research."

—HEINRICH ROHRER, "The Misconduct of Science"

"If you prick us do we not bleed? If you tickle us do we not laugh? If you poison us do we not die? And if you wrong us shall we not revenge?"

—WILLIAM SHAKESPEARE, *The Merchant of Venice*

"The nakedness of woman is the work of God."

—WILLIAM BLAKE, *Proverbs of Hell*

"Humiliation is the beginning of sanctification."

—JOHN DUNNE (ca. 1629)

The At-Your-Beck Felicity Conveyor

CHAPTER ONE

"There she is again, up to her brazen little snarfings," observed Justyce Dreadmiller, the neighborhood grocer. He followed this pouting young nymphet with his probing optics, unbeknownst to her, as she sauntered casually through the aisles, tossing seeming random staples into her shopping trolley whilst surreptitiously pocketing little luxury items from the pharmaceutical section—most likely (as per usual) sumptuous sex oils, fancy French perfumes, scented spermicidal lubricants, high-end beauty products and the like.

Mr. Dreadmiller considered himself a sensibly tolerant man and, more often than not, perfectly willing to "look the other way" rather than risk the bother of raising a big ruckus every time some wretched soul shoplifted an item or two from his food & drug library. After all, how many times was it, according to Jesus, that one should forgive one's brother for sinning against one? Was it seventy-seven times...? Was it seventy times seven times...? Or was it seventy times seven *plus* seven times...? That would be respectively 77, 490, and 497 times.

At this point Justyce Dreadmiller had lost track of the number of occasions this mischievous little trollop had stolen high-end merchandise from his store. He had acquired sufficient security footage to prove beyond a doubt (in court if need be) that she had given herself a five-finger discount from his market no less than 77 times, albeit with the statistical probability (if one tallied individual items versus the actual number of occasions she had trespassed against him) that it had been in excess of 497 times, over the past couple plus years.

This purse-proud entitlement princess sashayed into his business every couple days and never left without filching a fistful of high-ticket articles off his shelves. Where she stuffed her spoils was anybody's guess, what with the scandalously skimpy skirts she sported round the clock (even in the depths of winter on the face of it). Detaining her for a full body cavity strip search was absolutely out of the question, as it would like as not present formidable legal challenges, especially if it ended up being a non-consenting search that required cutting her clothing off with a scissors. He was concerned that such a scenario, were it to transpire, would potentially lead to all kinds of bureaucrappic rigamarole, not the least of which could land up being an extortionate lawsuit against his enterprise, wrongful or no.

He had neither the time nor energy to enter data into thousands of forms and questionaries containing subparagraph after subparagraph of convoluted legalese, bureaucratese, technobabble and whatnot in barely legible fine print that would be, according to his lights, unintelligible gobbledygook. Nor had he access to the financial resources that were requisite for hiring civil litigation attorneys on retainer to do all the paperwork in his behalf.

No sirree Bob. Not in *these* trousers...!

Justyce Dreadmiller was a man who valued simplicity and elegance. He believed, boots and all, in the virtue of solving his own problems in his own ways, on his own initiative, and at his own convenience, in as straightforward a manner as was practicable by whatever the proximate exigencies of the situation under scrutiny called for.

This, of course, didn't mean that his methods for resolving such issues would be entirely without embellishment, nor would they be devoid of discretionary leeway for spur-of-the-moment resolutions to be made by his dedicated minions, most of whom were trustworthy and dependable, even to the extent that he would grant them the freedom and flexibility to extemporize as they saw fit, especially when unforeseen circumstances arose that required breakneck decisions to be made unburdened by any statutory mandates to consult one's stuperiors (say, for example, in writing) beforehand. In this sense, Mr. Dreadmiller's management style was not unakin to that of your run-of-the-kill crime lords. He encouraged his employees to live by the motto: "Shoot first, ask questions later." All he really had to say to his hirelings was, "take care of it," and they would know *ex officio* exactly what needed to be done and would proceed forthwith to handle each and every problematic scenario in accordance with whatever the unique and distinctive contextual nuances happened to be that presented themselves within their unerring field of vision. Ninety-nine-point-nine percent of the time these little snags would be sorted out and set to rights with gentle nudges and friendly reminders, whilst in the other tenth of a percent of the time such setbacks and encumbrances would be ameliorated with politely rendered post-labor abortions. Not unnaturally, that was more in theory than in practice. For, in actual terms, although such matters were usually relatively painless to deal with, they were inevitably a lot messier than one might expect. And the running sore of this pestiferous little shoplifting Lolita was no exception to that general principle.

He had first taken note of this young lass's illicit undertakings back in the summer of 2021, when the COVID-19 pandemic had been raging out of control and he had found himself facing some serious challenges in his quest for qualified workers who could keep a proper eye on things. Let it suffice to recall that this particular epoch, in the recent collective memory of most American citizens, what with its bleach and toilet paper shortages and all, was a way far cry from what ordinary folk would fairly have considered as "golden times." Many of his workers had been hospitalized with this highly transmissible virus and a number of them had, regrettably, succumbed to it. Deeply saddened by the loss of some of his very best employees, Mr. Dreadmiller had felt it incumbent upon himself, in an effort to honor the memories of those who had given their lives to keep his business running, to strenuously take up the matter of rectifying the problem of this rapacious purloiner who kept on cabbaging his most valuable vendibles.

Although our enterprising entrepreneur had stumbled upon seeming insurmountable obstacles insofar as being able to clarify to himself, in explicitly rational terms, what the precise connection was between the tragic premature deaths of his employees from a murtherous respiratory virus and the chronically persistent delinquentations of this thieving little thoroughbred, he knew in his heart of hearts that the season had now arisen for him to "extract the fly from the ointment," as they say. On the surface these traumatic and unpleasant episodes may have appeared to be naught but strokes of ill luck, namely: unfurthersome (albeit fortuitous) quinky-dinks. Still and all, if one dug a little deeper into such matters, as Mr. Dreadmiller had with the unflagging diligence and oh-so methodical painstakingness of a long-range precision-strike missile engineer, 'twas all but inevitable, according to each and every inference drawn from his deductive albeit fallacious logic, that one would become accreasingly and unqualifiedly convinced to the point that one would no longer be able to help but extrapolate the inescapable conclusion of the ultra high statistical probability that one would eventually uncover an underlying connection between the deaths of his employees and the rampant thefts of his merchandise by this licentious little snatcher.

Mr. Dreadmiller had planned to do some renovations and technical upgrades to his store but the coronavirus pandemic had landed so heavily on his business that he had found himself in a financial pinch for the very first time subsequent to the grand opening of his grocery boutique back in the fall of 1999, at the tail end of the Clinton-Lewinsky debacle. He named the store after his beloved late granny (from the Oinkbladder side of the tribe), whose given name was "Mildred." His grocery boutique was thence called "Mildred's Market," which Mr. Dreadmiller thought had a nice homey, old-fashioned ring to it. Somehow or other the grandmotherly designation by itself lent to his enterprise a warm, welcoming, cozy, and comforting ambience.

Prior to the devastating onslaught of the COVID-19 pandemic in March, 2020, Mr. Dreadmiller had preserved just enough capital to invest in one of those fancy, high-end, high-tech, Japanese-manufactured belt conveying apparatuses, not dissimilar to the sushi trains in many Korean-owned Japanese eateries, though on a considerably more extravagant scale—something not unakin to an airport baggage carousel, albeit with a host of extra super-fancy accessories. It was a belting machine of sorts, called (in English) an "At-Your-Beck Felicity Conveyor," that was designed and constructed to serve not just the fish and meat sections of a market but every other square inch thereof into the bargain. There were, for example, these nifty little automated multi-functional spoons, forks, and boning, paring, and carving knives that could apportion precise measurements of customized ingredients into bottles and bags according to the explicit specifications of each individual patron. This ingenious apparatus also included many pendulous and lateral accessories that could execute virtually any cogitable task and render thereby the subjectively mundane experience of grocery shopping immensely more enjoyous and convenient. And the nice thing about it was that most of these accessories were discretionary insomuch as they could be ordered smack dab as our enterprising entrepreneur saw fit whensoever the need arose for a replacement or improvement.

The choices of accessories at one's disposal were seeming without limit. They included, for example, miniature hanging hose-pipes and atomizers wherewith to spray specifically selected produce at meticulously timed intervals; meat pounders of all shapes and sizes for tenderizing beef, pork, and other ambrosial aliments; automated soap, water, and sanitizer dispensers to afford customers the option of wiping and/or washing their hands & feet (at no extra cost) when and whithersoever they desired; mechanized straps and robo-buckles that locked receptacles of any size, shape, and form to the belt until they were rubber-stamped and purchased with authorized platinum cards (a star feature that had already proved, upon undergoing tens of thousands of product tests, to be dramatically effective in reducing incidencies of latrocination and/or armed stickups); not to mention medium voltage electrical shocks that would be administered from invisible fences around certain perishable items (and confectionery goods in particular) to discourage unattended toddlers from touching or ingesting them.

So amazingly versatile was this apparatus, in fact, that it was possible to alter its overall function at the mere flick of a switch (or turn of a dial, as the case may be). By way of example, it could be transmogrified into a full-service gambling casino, replete with slot machines, big six wheels, video lottery terminals and suchlike, or it could be morphed into a funfair-style horror train ride with all the requisite holograms of boogeymen, gargoyles, science-fiction monsters and whatnot. With this in mind, Mr. Dreadmiller considered applying to the city for a license to open his market on weekend nights to function as a family-friendly entertainment venue of sorts. Indeed, the possibilities for upgrading his business were seeming without end!

Consequently, it goes without saying that, in light of our resourceful and conscientious entrepreneur fostering a compelling desire to offer his devoted patrons the very best-of-the-best and most up-to-the-minute creature comforts, pleasurable diversions, and recreational amenities that were practicable within the constraints of his annual budget, Mr. Justyce Dreadmiller was dead set upon purchasing and installing this nifty new appliance into his grocery boutique. And it was, in particular, this hyper-sensitivity, on his part, to the needs and desires of his customers that kept them unswervingly loyal insomuch as they would return to his store time and time again, notwithstanding the fact that there were some half-dozen larger and more impersonal mega-corporate supermarket wholesale houses just a few short blocks away from his boutique that offered many of the same items he did at competitively marked-down bargain-basement discount prices. The costs of such items at these superstores were so dirt cheap in comparison with those at his own store, in fact, that Mr. Dreadmiller himself ended up doing most of his personal household shopping at such chains, apart from the fact that he disrelished the very sight of them. To preclude the commissioning by our grocer of what would likely be perceived by his disciples as acts of high treason from being uncovered by potential anonymous (never mind non-anonymous) whistleblowers, he would either have to disguise himself with a pair of Groucho goggles (consisting of an oversize plastic nose, a large black caterpiller of a mustache, and eyebrows to match) or would simply dress up as a dignified old maid with rouged lips, powdered cheeks, navy blue mascara, and a dead bird on his head to avoid being caught red-handed violating his own highest principles (specifically, unwritten codes for members of the landed gentry eligible for inclusion in the Social Register) insofar as the class of establishments went to which he chose to bring his business. It was not unlike, say, the King of England dressed as Lady Gaga shopping at Walmart, or a sworn effete classical music snob in a MAGA hat shouting "USA! USA! USA!" in unison with thousands of others at a political rally booming with rockabilly band music (and/or other quasi paranormal phenomena along similar such lines).

Be that as it may, as sure as shit stinks, after closing shop later that evening, when Mr. Dreadmiller compiled a careful inventory of the female products lining the shelves in the pharmaceutical section of his store, the usual suspected cosmetic items, sex toys and whatnot turned up short. His computations revealed that he had lost over seven-hundred dollars worth of inventory on that very day, which was worse than usual whenever this delinquent little skirt walked off with his wares. He had calculated that, over the past two and a half years or so, he had either lost or misplaced some ninety-thousand dollars worth of inventory, and all this was on account of the artful machinations of this twinkle-toed little nightbird. He figured, therefore, that it was high time he took his Lord and Savior up on the more liberal interpretation of that pesky verse in Matthew that implied (at least, according to his own biblical exegesis thereof) that one should desist from forgiving one's brother (or, in this case, one's sister) if sinned against *more* than 77 times.

If this entitled little *Schulmädchen* had, alternatively, been a poor slovenly old bag lady pilfering from his shelves a cheap can of tuna, a low-grade jar of peanut butter or whatever, he would never have so much as even batted an eye, for he adjudged himself a man of profound empathy and deepfelt compassion for those less fortunate than he, and perstood extremely well, from the difficult circumstances in which he himself had been raised as a child, how incredibly cutthroat the competition was when one had no choice but to drag oneself up by one's own bootstraps, as *he* most assuredly had—*yes sirree!*

Mr. Justyce Dreadmiller considered himself the quintessential self-made man and was glad and proud to have founded and managed a highly acclaimed grocery boutique (as indicated by its Yelp ratings) in the very heart of the upscale neighborhood of Pimpleton Heights, which was a comfortably affluent suburb of the greater Pimpleton retropolitan area, where he had grown up from early childhood and eventually come of age. His own unique rise from abject poverty (having been raised in a broken home with thirteen siblings) to upper middle-class prosperity had both affirmed the Horatio Alger rags-to-riches theory that hard work does indeed pay off and belied it insomuch as Mr. Dreadmiller himself had never sucked up to any wealthy benefactors to pave his way to financial well-being. (The trumped-up rags-to-riches narrative was symptomatic of an outmoded mindset that most Americans nowadays considered naught but romantic mythology of the most queasily saccharine sort.) On top of all that, he was pleased to count himself blissfully wed and abundantly blessed insomuch as he had managed, with his loving (and lovely) wife, to have raised two beautiful well-mannered children—a son and a daughter—both of whom had managed to grow up gracefully and get accepted into notable institutions of higher earning through naught but their own sweat & grit. It would thus be no oversell to say that Mr. Dreadmiller's vicarious pride in his children's achievements was in no way whatsoever delusional. Indeed, his son and daughter were both intrepid pioneers in their chosen areas of expertise and were fast gaining respect and recognition from not just their immediate peers but also from internationally acknowledged experts in their fields.

As for Justyce Dreadmiller himself, he was relatively well off and had, for many years, made a good solid upper-middle-class income from his honest hard work as a neighborhood merchant. Indeed, 'twould be no exaggeration to say that he represented the very embodiment of old-line upward mobility. He was its poster boy, no less.

Be all that as it might, no matter how one looked at it, $90,000.00 wasn't exactly "chump change." He had two kids in college to support, a monthly mortgage to pay on his suburban-style McMansion, and, on top of everything else, there were imminent health concerns in the family that required extensive medical attention and occasional emergency visits to the hospital that ate up huge chunks of his hard-earned income. Moreover, he had only recently finalized his decision to purchase the aforesaid Felicity Conveyor for his shop and, on account of being short on funds, had no choice but to buy it on a payment schedule that required monthly installments with extortionately high interest rates that were, for him (as things presently stood), barely sustainable, especially when taking under account his already massive overhead.

It had thus only recently occurred to Mr. Dreadmiller that if he had nipped things in the bud from the very start, with respect to this shameless young strumpet who purloined his inventory as if on cruise control, he would never have found himself in a situation where he'd be compelled to pay such usurious borrowing rates on this must-have appliance but instead would have been able to purchase it out of pocket, with zero interest payments and no questions asked, had he not found himself ninety-thousand dollars short on funds. Thus, what had started out as an annoying little inconvenience had now become, from his point of view, the proverbial "match in the powder keg."

Mr. Dreadmiller figured, for that reason, that the hour had now come for him to square his accounts with this opulent little klepto who kept taking from him and who, apart from everything else, didn't seem to have a care in the world, what with a certain *je ne sais quoi* and procacious air of nonchalance she exuded whensoever she awaited her turn at the checkout counter, which exasperated him no end. In despite of her outward show of mannerliness—"A good morrow to thee, sir!" "Thank you ever so much!" "Take good care, monsieur!" "Have a beautiful day!"—she was, to him, the omniperfect epitome of barefaced impudence. He reckoned that if he did nothing at all to address this ongoing issue, it might eventually escalate into something much worse, something he would no longer be able to manage or control, especially were he to gain a reputation neighborhoodwise (howsoever unintentionally) of being a humbuggable old poopbutt who simply turned a blind eye whenever some nefarious soul cavalierly ripped him off. The prospect of his store attracting flash mobs that would execute full-scale smash-and-grabs of his invaluable vendibles kept him broad awake most nights, tossing & turning, which accounted for the heavy bags under his optics that had formed in recent months.

What most individuals failed to realize, however, is that just because someone was nice didn't mean they were stupid. Even nice people were capable of committing cold-blooded murder if certain marks were overstepped. And Mr. Dreadmiller was sufficiently self-aware to know, beyond a doubt, that he was no exception to that fundamental principle of the human equation. What distinguished Mr. Dreadmiller from most other people was that, while he had the sufferance of a saint, he also had the temper of a wolverine, but, unlike wolverines, he was able to keep his temper in check, under a cloak of mild-mannered innoxiousness, until the right moment presented itself for the efficacious implementation of punitive reprisals against his mortal enemies, which gave him time aplenty to plot his revengeances against anyone he perceived as having wronged or slighted him in any way whatsoever he adjudged to be signally excuseless, hence unforgivable.

Of course, it goes without saying that unprovoked acts of aggression would be rigorously reviewed by a non-partisan panel to determine if they exceeded a particular standard that would justify an appropriate redressal of aggrievances by agressees to ensure that all playing fields, as it were, would be properly re-leveled. A rigorous twelve-point questionnaire would needs must be filled out, signed, and reviewed by a committee that would determine if a complaint against a given unprovoked aggressor passed muster. *Intent* always played an important role in such cases to establish the appropriate recompense for an unprovoked act of aggression.

Mr. Dreadmiller had, by way of illustration (subsequent to having filled out all the conveniable forms, having had them duly notarized at the point of appending his signature to them, dotting all his i's & crossing all his t's, fret cetera, sweat cetera) engineered a well-deserved comeuppance for an aggressive bully at his prep school who had once thrown his briefcase out of a second-story window onto a rooftop during his sophomore geometry class. In this case a boundary had been exceeded from which there was no turning back, as determined by a unanimous vote of the non-partisan panel that reviewed the case, especially given the fact that the bully in question had never even bothered to kneel down in abject submission with his schnozzle to the soil in a steaming pile of Herr Justyce Dreadmiller's pet mastiff's diarrhoea to mournfully beg his forgiveness, accompanied by a sincere offer to make unconditional restitution to him for having so belligerently trespassed against him, which clemency Herr Justyce Dreadmiller would (in theory, at least) have been more than happy and willing to vouchsafe, for he was a man of great empathy, tolerance, compassion, and good will. So just, good, and forgiving was he by nature that he was invariably inclined to give any soul suspected of wronging him in the worst possible way the benefit of the doubt (i.e. *in dubio pro reo*).

Without needing to go into all the grisly details of how Mr. Dreadmiller had, in due course, gone about settling his score with said bully, let it suffice to recount that, exactly six years to the day following the aforetold briefcase disturbance, the bully in question awakened one morning, woozy from an elevated dose of Phenobarbital mixed with Rohypnol and Ketamine, to find himself naked as a maggot in a ditch hundreds of miles away from his home, in the middle of a pestilential, snake-infested swamp, in the most excruciating cogitable psychophysiological agony from having just undergone the crudest of all orchiectomies in conjunction with an even cruder penectomy that had been executed, as all the evidence had suggested, by an unlicensed surgeon who had used a rusty old dagger to make all the necessary (and unnecessary) cuts & incisions, together with a generous dose of sulphuric acid as a topical "anti-anaesthetic" (or pain-intensifier) that had left collateral third-degree chemical burns all over said bully's body, including his face, which is now permanently disfigured and resistant to any known cosmetic surgical treatments. The remains of his penis and testicles were found near the ditch half-eaten by worms, snakes, and vultures. A fully charged traceable burner phone was left with the unseminared bully as a compassionate act of untold kindness & mercy (a supreme testament to the fundamental humanity of the bully's chosen prey). When the authorities found the capsized bully, he was immediately medevaced by whirly-bird (at his own expense, of course) to a nearby hospital, where he was treated for his wounds (without health insurance) for the next six and a half months. He survived (albeit barely) and is—so far as Mr. Dreadmiller was able to ascertain by means of the subterranean conduits of classified intelligence accessed by his close friends and allies on the city council (specifically: Herr Doktors Lobotocelli, Ampukoviç, and Sawitov, who currently preside over the psychosexual surgical wing of Mount Sade General Hospital in the heart of downtown Pimpleton)—still having his weekly paychecks garnished for the medical bills he owes the hospital some thirty-plus years after having been disciplined by Mr. Dreadmiller for his egregious misconduct.

The bully currently makes a "living" as a part-time cleaning attendant at a hog farm on the outskirts of the city, where he's paid a modest honorarium to sweep up and dispose of inedible offal as well as to process tons of swine manure into fertilizer by means of antiquated composting methods. The bully is permitted only to work night shifts on account of the deformed facial features he now possesses that were caused by the sulphuric acid therapy he'd received on the night of his penalization—a therapy that served to accentuate his already monstrous physical appearance. Upon being discharged from the hospital, the hog farm turned out to be the only establishment in town willing to take him on as a part-time employee, albeit with the strongest of reservations due to his repulsive physical appearance. He was given no choice but to sign a contract that obliged him to promise—under threat of facing solitary confinement at ADX Florence (otherwise known as the "Alcatraz of the Rockies") in the event that he failed to comply with said directive— that he would work only night shifts and never show his unsightly map to any of the hog farm's customers or employees during business hours, lest it curdle their blood and frighten them off to seek employment and/or take their business elsewhere.

Since the time of his release from the hospital the bully has managed to sustain himself on the only fringe benefit his employment at the hog farm provides him, namely: the scraps of quasi-edible offal he sweeps off the floors every night, which he takes home to his tenement studio in the skid-row section of Pimpleton's east-side ghetto to cook for himself in the weest hours of the morn, just prior to the peep of day.

In any case, as far as Mr. Dreadmiller was concerned, that was all water under the bridge, seeing as he had been able within minutes to recover his briefcase un-blemished off the rooftop upon which it had been casually tossed. Had his briefcase or its content been harmed in any way whatsoever, the retributive consequences for said offendant would have been incrementally more severe.

Upon conjuring in his mind the three allegedly wise monkeys of the famous Japanese pictorial maxim who "see no evil, hear no evil, speak no evil," Herr Justyce Dreadmiller's soul case thrummled with a savage resentment that had seethed inside him for the past thirty-plus years. "Not on your Nelly!" thought he, harrumphing to himself in a low susurration. "Enough of such ackamarackus!" He had come to be up to his ears in such hooey-balooey and decided then and there, on the spot, that he would never again permit himself ever to be duped by the philosophical creed expressed by this proverbial aphorism. It was time for him to open up his eyes, perk up his ears, and warm up his vocal cords, for he was fed up through and through with this facinorous little fly-by-night taking advantage of him and, by extension, his hard-working employees and dedicated patrons!

First of all, Mr. Dreadmiller had taken note from the very start that this (admittedly) stunningly attractive young *fille de joie* would strut into his store decked out in what appeared to be the type of ludicrously expensive designer duds that only the filthiest of the filthy rich could afford. One day it was a Balmain Women's 2-Pocket Belted Leather Trapeze Miniskirt, which runs in most catalogues for no less than $3,000.00. On another occasion she sashayed insouciantly into his boutique accoutered in a Grommet Embroidered Leather Mini Skater Skirt, which runs for $8,500.00.

The reader may wonder how Mr. Dreadmiller could be so well-versed in such matters, especially for a man in his line of work. Well, it turned out that his daughter Celine was studying to become a fashion designer at the ultra prestigious Pimpleton Heights Academy of Art & Design, and was, for that reason, inclined to share with him her boundless—and, dare it be said, contagious—enthusiasm apropos of the field in which she was fast gaining professional expertise, a branch of knowledge that was totally at odds with Mr. Dreadmiller's day-to-day business priorities. Wanting to please his beautiful daughter, nevertheless, by demonstrating an interest in her passions, he walked the extra mile that any loving progenitor would to conduct his own research on the fashion industry in his spare hours. That being said, he was proud of his little angel, as any parent would be, for Celine had turned out to be a perfectly lovely young lady. She was quick on the draw, smart as a whip, and up to the dodge, and, most importantly (at least from his fatherly perspective), she was a kind, faithful, loving, and dutiful daughter.

Well, to Mr. Dreadmiller's way of thinking, the point, as it pertained to the cunning little hoister who kept returning to his store, revolved around the enigmatic mind-boggler as to why in the world such an exquisite looking adolescent lady (as this compulsive klepto unarguably was) would wish to squander her precious time and energy, and even risk her reputation (if she had one to defend), by boosting vendibles from the shelves of his enterprise when she was, by all manner of evidence, well-heeled enough to lawfully procure anything she desired without, apparently, having to break the bank to do so. Could it be, peradventure, that the light-fingered proclivity of this debauched young seductress was entangled with some deep-seated, self-destructive psycho-emotional issues hearkening back to, say, a maladjusted, adversity-filled childhood? An abusive upbringing, belikes? Was she, by chance, stealing symbolically the unconditional love she never received from her wardens? Did this young demoiselle originate, haps, from one of those pro-verbial dysfunctional rich families one reads about *ad nauseam* in the supermarket tabloids...?

Now, these were questions he had already asked himself many months before, so it wasn't as though he hadn't already taken the time to do his homework in a conscious, rigorous, and determined effort to gather whatever intelligence he was able to coherently assemble on this little girl's sociocultural background, her family pedigree, her criminal records (if any), and other such things. "Yvette Cartier" was her moniker (quite a pretty one, he thought), as he had easily ascertained from the stacks of credit card receipts he had accrued over the years, which he stored for safe-keeping inside his walk-in freezer at home. Her curfew keepers, it turned out, were distinguished faculty members at Pimpleton State Luniversity, which Mr. Dread-miller's son Eiden attended. Her father's area of expertise, apparently, was Dia-lectical Hermeneutics and her mother was a tenured Professor of Psychopathology (figures, he thought). Having researched their salaries, it was evident that, although the girl's parents were warm-pocketed, much as Mr. Dreadmiller himself was (most of the time, at least), they weren't exactly what one would call "rolling in it" (as neither was he), though he had fadged out from extensive investigations into their finances (largely with the assistance of certain casual acquaintances of his on the city council who recurrently got wind of all the regional high-society viceversations and clish-ma-claver) that there was a significant amount of cash flowing in via a trust fund from the girl's adoptive great uncle, who was a well-known war-profiteering oil tycoon from the Deep South called "Harmon Ebenoid Weaser," a man who had once run as a gubernatorial candidate in one of the low-lying southeastern states as well as for a Republican seat in the Senate. This man apparently had a special thing for his great niece insofar as most of the cabbage from the trust fund flowed directly into her private bank accounts (a good number of which were offshore in Singapore, Switzerland, Hong Kong, Panama, and the Cayman Islands). Interest-ingly, Mademoiselle Cartier had been adopted by her parents—let's call them her guardians then—when she was eleven years of age, which might account for certain aspects of her psycho-moral dysfunction that would have led to this otherwise in-explicable kleptomaniacal streak of hers. Whilst Mr. Dreadmiller considered it of paramount importance to gain credible insights into the motivating mechanisms underpinning this girl's psychopathological make-up, it had zero effect whatsoever in as far as persuading him to harbor even so much as an ounce of sympathy for her egregious criminal behavior.

Now, it's been said, according to the theory of Six Degrees of Separation, that all people are only six or fewer social connections away from one another. Well, as it turned out, Mr. Dreadmiller's son Eiden happened to be a close friend of a young man called Werther Nemesinovich who had once had the hots for Yvette Cartier when they were in prep school together, and had even dated her for several months until she dumped him like a hot potato after conning him out of his summer's earnings from a back-breaking day job at the local sewage treatment plant for a pair of Blue Nile diamond stud earrings from Tiffany's. The young man was so deeply traumatized by this rejection of his overtures—that is to say, "overtures" in the sense that she had never even allowed the poor fellow so much as a peck on her cheek (much less her netherlips)—that he had found himself on the verge of casting himself off a bridge tower, into the local river, until his good friend Eiden (bless his heart and soul!) had heroically dissuaded him from doing so.

After a day or two of thoughtful reflection, Mr. Dreadmiller decided to disclose to his son, and his unfurthersome buddy Werther, the left-handed feats he had witnessed (not to mention filmed and videographed) perpetrated by Ms. Cartier at Mildred's Market over the past couple-plus years. Although Eiden and Werther were shocked by the film and video footage he had shared with them, which included some high-resolution film tracks featuring scenes, in lush technicolor, of this unrepentant tart purloining upmarket items off his shelves in broad daylight, they were, at the same time, not the least bit surprised to learn that such unconscionable behavior would emanate from aforesaid source. The harrowing tragedy of scornful rejection and wallet humping to which Werther had been subjugated by this unapologetic prickteaser tallied well with Mr. Dreadmiller's comprehensive behavioral assessment of Ms. Cartier's overarching moral character.

As it turned out, both Werther and Eiden had, by sheer coincidence, already conducted their *own* detailed investigations of this presumptuous young winklot and had managed independently to dig up some powerful dirt apropos of certain other of this artful young lady's unadmonished misdoings. As it so happened, they had ascertained from reliable sources that Ms. Cartier had developed a pernicious habit of buying academic papers from a host of term paper mills online and elsewhere. In more recent years she had even gone so far as to hire a local ghostwriter on retainer to do most, if not all, of her school assignments in her behalf, the effectuation of which amounted to nothing short of full-fledged academic fraud, which, in and of itself, although no cause for imprisonment per se, had the inherent potential, all the same, to land this young lady in a world of trouble.

Justyce Dreadmiller, a beacon of positivity and protector of local traditions, who was unanimously beloved for his charitable acts of kindness and good works in the community, and who was thereby viewed as a highly valued denizen thereof, was eminently well-connected to the point of being on a first-name basis with many of the most powerful and influential personages in the region. He was, in point of fact, frequently invited to their cocktail and dinner parties as an honored guest. Well, as it turned out, he happened to be a close friend of Ulrich Armstrong, who was Dean & President of Pimpleton State Luniversity, a high-ranking educational institution attended not only by his son Eiden but also, providentially, by Yvette Cartier.

Justyce Dreadmiller decided then and there to give his old buddy a call to suggest a rendezvous with him and his wife Helga for a drink after work on Wednesday evening. Howbeit, instead of meeting at the Skunk & Barnacle Brewpub downtown, just catty-corner across from the Hall of Injustice (which had always been their favorite stomping ground), Professor Armstrong invited Herr Dreadmiller to the cordial intimacy of his stately old home on the hill overlooking the city.

CHAPTER TWO

"So wonderful to see you again, my dear old friend!" said Ulrich Armstrong as he gave Justyce Dreadmiller a big warm bear hug. "Come in, come in! Make yourself at home. How 'bout a drink? I've got an unopened bottle of BHAKTA 1946 Armagnac—a very fine French concoction. It's described in the accompanying brochure as showing 'brioche, salted caramel, and forest floor on the nose, followed by apple crumble, cigar box, and licorice on the palate.' Whaddya think?"

"I very much appreciate your kindness and generosity, Ulrich, but I don't wish to impose upon you and your wife. A simple craft beer would do me just fine."

"But my friend," replied Ulrich Armstrong, "how often do we get to see one another? Even though you live no more than two or three miles away from us, our worldly existences have gotten so inextricably entangled with the unavoidable vicissitudes of life, it seems we haven't been able to visit each other in years. Life's short. I insist, without further ado, that we celebrate this occasion whilst we still have an opportunity to do so!"

"Ulrich, of course!" said Mr. Dreadmiller, upon realizing that his old buddy was spot-on. "I consider you one of my closest friends and allies. I shall accept your magnanimous offer with humble gratitude. Armagnac it shall be!"

After warming themselves up with snifters of this rare vintage of brandy and exchanging the usual formalities and small talk, Justyce Dreadmiller got down to the point of his visit. From his valise he produced several high-quality reels of film footage and thumb drives containing video clips he had earlier shown to his son Eiden, and his son's friend Werther, of the wayward young coed named Yvette Cartier, who happened to be a freshman at the school that Ulrich Armstrong was known to administrate with what was described by those abreast of the facts as "an iron fist in a velvet glove" (a description which was, in and of itself, an air-brushed euphemism that only served to belie the bona fide disciplinary intensity wherewith the school's multifarious departments & programs were superintended by his old chum).

The footage revealed unequivocal videographic evidence of Mademoiselle Cartier's illicit appropriations of valuable cosmetic merchandise from Mr. Dreadmiller's shelves, amounting, over the past two and a half years (as he divulged to his friend), to an estimated $90,000.00 in damage from uninsured losses of his inventory. Our resourceful and enterprising store owner had enlisted the help of one of the senior faculty members from the motion picture department of the Pimpleton Heights

Academy of Art & Design to edit down the footage and incorporate therewithin strategic freeze frames highlighting the various sleight-of-hand tricks practiced by this cunning little sex kitten whilst in the act of pilfering top-line wares off the shelves of his boutique. Much in the manner of a power-point presentation, he went on to explain to President Armstrong the extent to which these pilferings were starting to impede his ability to afford the technical upgrades he wished to install in his business to improve customer service and maintain customer loyalty. He mentioned, in particular, his urgent need (with an eye to future-proofing his business) to securing the acquisition of the Japanese-manufactured appliance known as an "At-Your-Beck Felicity Conveyor," replete with a thousand-and-one luxurious accessories. He explained to his friend that, in order to stay competitive in today's market, it was imperative that he "keep up with the Joneses," especially as he would never be able to mark down his merchandise to the bargain basement discount prices that the mega-corporate supermarket chains near him were able to offer their clientele.

Professor Ulrich Armstrong drew a deep frown upon viewing the videographic footage of Ms. Cartier's thievish undertakings. Students at his school were not only expected to maintain high grade-point averages but also to conduct themselves off campus with proper modesty and decorum in a manner that upheld the luniversity's unimpeachable reputation for not just academic but moral excellence withal.

After a magnificent and memorable evening of long awaited camaraderie (reminiscing about the good old days and such) with Ulrich and his wife Helga, Justyce Dreadmiller motored back home feeling considerably more at peace with himself than he had for many months prior thereto, seeing as how he had gained the reassurances of his good old friend—the powerful dean & president of Pimpleton State—that he and his wife would initiate forthwith an independent investigation into this morally lax young lady, who was evidently in dire need of some exacting penitential discipline. Justyce Dreadmiller had also relayed to his friend—albeit with greater reluctance, as he hadn't yet gained into his possession conclusive documentary evidence thereof—the matters brought up by Eiden and Werther appertaining to Mademoiselle Cartier's purported commissioning of incontrovertible academic fraud. He was confident, all the same, that everything would eventually sort itself out.

Professor Armstrong's wife Helga had also watched the video footage of this scheming young tart and heard the allegations of academic dishonesty with elevated interest, especially as she was a close friend of Yvette's governess Prunelda, whom she had known since grammar school. She begged her husband's permission to go speak with her friend on this delicate matter.

It was heartening for Mr. Dreadmiller to finally feel, with a renewed sense of confidence, that the starter motors were beginning to crank the engines of the judicial machinery, which would, ere long, chug up at a steady clip. The truth would eventually be out, fairness achieved, justice served, and long overdue comeuppances delivered to their rightful wrongdoer.

CHAPTER THREE

O n being unexpectedly asked out on a date one morning in late November, Yvette Cartier, who loved taking advantage of vulnerable young men, met with Werther's old buddy Eiden at her favorite restaurant later that evening —an Icelandic Sudanese bistro known for its innovative avant-garde cuisine. As Eiden and his father had anticipated, Yvette ordered the most expensive items on the menu, including several bottles of wine, from which she drank only a mouthful, fully expecting Eiden to pay every penny of the bill. With a well-nigh clairvoyant perspicacity as to what needed to be done ahead of time, Justyce Dreadmiller, Werther Nemesinovich, President Ulrich Armstrong and his wife Helga had all pitched in for the foreboded expenses of Eiden's evening out with this saucy young minx.

"So prithee tell me, Yvette," asked Eiden, in a determined effort to break the awkward silence at the power display table at which they were seated, "what field of study are you focused on at the moment?"

This adolescent lady, with her undulating sinuous waves of silky dark hair and radiant rosy complexion, was devastatingly, nay, transcendently beautiful by any standard wherewith feminine beauty could be measured, so it was no wonder that Eiden empathized wholeheartedly with Werther's insane, almost blind, infatuation for this girl, for he too found himself mesmerized by the lithe curves of her physique and exquisite perfection of her facial bone structure. It appeared as though Yvette had no need or desire whatsoever to make any kind of conscious effort to so much as feign, let alone pretend, to be the least bit couthie or congenial, even though it was costing three families an arm and a leg to take her out to this pretentious marked up meal in a restaurant that had obviously (to him, at least) been over-aggrandized by self-appointed cuisine critics, toffee-nosed culinary judges, self-important epicurean connoisseurs, hoity-toity foodies, highfalutin hipsters, and all the rest. It could not but be concluded, therefore, that, taking into account her unapproachable standoffishness under such circumstances, Mademoiselle Cartier was a far cry *in extremis* from what one would fairly call "outgoing" or "gregarious." Whilst, on the one hand, she came across as being ingenuously modest and reserved, even disarmingly self-conscious by dint of her demurely downcast countenance, this feeling was belied (not unmarkedly so, in fact) by the seductive leather micro miniskirt she was sporting—the kind of haute couture fashion amongst the young, beautiful, and super-filthy rich whereby it was formidably challenging, if not flat out impossible, to discern if your straight-from-central-casting, banged-up-to-the-mark modern teenage schoolgirl a-go-go was wearing anything whatsoever subjacent thereto, what with all the intermittent peekaboos of exposed bottomcheeks and southern-most regions of bum cracks and such one typically associates with aforesaid articles of raiment. At max, she may have been wearing one of those side-tie G-strings that were, for the nonce, all the rage. He wondered, however, if she was merely waiting for him to make an aggressive move on her by allotting him the incredibly narrow window of opportunity that young women in her league now and then accorded boy-toys like himself, which usually didn't last longer than a nanosecond (give or take) and tended to pass from sight in a whiff, like the tantalic undulations and come-hither glowings of a pulsating Fata Morgana.

The fact that Yvette had so much as even deigned to vouchsafe Eiden her precious time of day seemed, in her mind (he assumed), to suffice on her end of the social contract. Eiden, unlike his friend Werther, possessed a high enough level of self-confidence not to be seduced by this girl in terms of feeling any kind of romantic attraction for her, but felt, on the contrary, a compelling desire to give her a firm spanking—not one of those lame little sconings customarily administered by British headmasters over the skirts of misbehaved schoolgirls in the guarded privacy of their stuffy little office chambers (doors locked, shades drawn and all), but rather a brisk bare-naked spanking in a cool breezy crowded public outdoor arena attended by a large and appreciative audience of stern, exacting, and uncompromising disci-plinarians—and their chuckling, giggling offspring to boot!

"I'm as yet undecided," she answered inscrutably, without any effort to create a bridge for further conversation.

Eiden, who was wired up to the teeth, knew he had to keep this little chit-chat rolling in order to milk his subject for any useful intelligence relating to her villainous acts and wicked ways and, perhaps, plant a seed or two in her presump-tively impressionable young mind to motivate her sinistrous instincts and enhance therethrough the marginal likelihood that she would eventually let her guard down and either say or do, or say & do, something retchless or stuntly (or both) with the object of ensuring that she would sooner or later be caught in flagrante delicto either committing an offense point-blank and/or confessing to having committed one (with all the gruesome details explicitly laid out by her so that they could be cross-referenced in the wee hours of the morn by several dozen teams of profes-sional investigators), such that she would be rendered legally eligible to be charged with a criminal offense.

"On another subject," said Eiden, moving forward suavely, "I have an older sister who's majoring in Fashion at the Pimpleton Heights Academy of Art & Design. I cannot help but observe that you dress exceptionally stylishly and, moreover, in a manner that, in my humble stupinion, not only bespeaks but also embodies the very epitome of fine taste and impeccable breeding. My sister Celine, by the bye, is on a first name basis with Giorgo Armani, Donatella Versace, Karl Lagerfeld,

Ralph Lauren, Calvin Klein, and a host of other renowned fashion designers and couturiers. She also receives a prodigious abundance of perquisites as an influencer on the rise—free designer shoes, skirts, dresses, raincoats and whatnot—just by her amicable association with such rich and powerful celebrities. I imagine the two of you would get on famously. Indeed, I would be delighted and honored to introduce you to Celine ... that is to say, if you're interested in meeting her."

For the first time that evening Eiden detected a spark of non-aloofness in Yvette's striking physiognomy that lit up her resplendently beautiful eyes. Mr. Dreadmiller's son, known by his friends to be a smooth talker, felt confident that Yvette would take the bait. As a departure from the usual, she cracked an understated smile at him—not a fake smile, as there was no discernible absence of movement in the outer portion of the muscles orbiting her eyes, but rather a warm and genuine one.

"Your sister sounds like a fascinating person," she said. "I'd love to meet her sometime."

That was the icebreaker that made Yvette more willing to open up and make casual conversation with Eiden. It didn't hurt, too, that the three families involved in exposing her misdoings pitched in for the expense of renting a Ferrari for the week. After dinner, when they both felt more relaxed, Eiden drove her to a quiet cul-de-sac bordering the trailhead of a local city park and brought the conversation around to her academic studies once again in an effort to gather further intelligence on her fraudulent practices. He made note that she was vague and elusive when discussing her intellectual pursuits and scholarly attainments. He played along and claimed that he, too, was undecided about which subjects to focus on in school, having not yet declared a major (which was a bald-faced lie). Such false confessions of his congenital indecisiveness in school constituted a masterfully executed ploy to disarm his subject with the aim of increasing the likelihood that she would let her guard down. He confided to her (falsely) that he had once hired a ghostwriter to compose his term papers and do hundreds of other school assignments for him as well. None of these things were true, of course, as Eiden was nothing if not a stellar straight-A student of unimpeachable academic integrity.

Yvette appeared to be genuinely warming up to her date, sitting cozily with him in the passenger seat of what she was led to believe was Eiden's very own $600,000.00 Ferrari SF90 Spider coupe. What his poor friend Werther had been unable to achieve in many months' time Eiden already knew by instinct he could achieve on his very first date with this breathtakingly gorgeous young demoiselle. Although it was tempting to lean over and steal a kiss from her, he exerted himself to stay focused on his mission and did everything in his power not to permit himself to succumb to the wily flirtations of this dangerous temptress. Instead, he communicated unconsciously through his body language that he was "in to having a thing with her," and she appeared to reciprocate his prompts with her own non-verbal responses.

To maintain the conversational flow, he asked her, out of the blue, if she happened to have a part-time McJob to support her college tuition and housing expenses. Yvette confessed that she didn't have a McJob but that her guardians had been nagging her to death to go find one. From their point of view it wasn't just a matter of earning one's keep but also of building up one's character and gaining experience in the "real world," as they styled it. Also, working at a menial drudge job was, according to her guardians, instructive insofar as it motivated one to work harder in school with an eye to avoiding the pitfall of having to do dead-end jobs for the duration of one's natural life subsequent to making careless decisions and poor choices or, simply put, fatal missteps at the peak of one's formative years.

"I know a place," said Eiden, "where there's a great McJob opening that requires virtually no work at all (or work experience for that matter) and pays leagues beyond any minimum-wage job. All you really have to do is just sit around and read a book and/or diddle on your tardphone for the entirety of the shift with nothing more expected from you than picking up and taking messages once in a blue moon whenever the landline happens to ring—which is practically never!"

"Wow!" replied Yvette, "that sounds like the ideal dream job for me!" Her countenance lit up with a flicker of what appeared to be genuine non-indifference. "If I could get a McJob like that I'd be able to feed two, maybe even three, birds with one scone. Do you know where I can apply for this post?"

"It's right next door to Mildred's Market downtown," said Eiden, "the grocery boutique on the corner of Fifth Street & Main...? You would be working for a small firm there that specializes in the warehousing, sales, and distribution of ultra-expensive cosmetics, exotic perfumes, bottles of sex odors, and other stuff like that."

Now Yvette's eyes effervesced with an even brighter spark of excitement. "Eiden, that sounds absolutely perfect for me! Thank you so much in advance for this valuable information. You're a life saver!"

At this point in the conversation, things had heated up a bit until Yvette made a surprise move on her date. Catching Eiden completely off guard, she reached over and kissed him wetly on the lips. When he opened his mouth to speak, her tongue insinuated itself into his box of ivories. There was a sudden and acute spark of electrical momentum between the two of them. Much as he aspired to stay in control, he found her all but impossible to gainstrive, so he played along with the flow of the moment, even pretending to be shaky and nervous at times, as though he were somehow emotionally involved and vulnerable (girls in general liked that sort of thing in a man, as he'd learnt from prior experience) and also as if he truly cared about whether or not she would fancy spending time with him again.

If Eiden had been completely honest with himself, he would have realized on the spot that he was far more susceptible to being seduced by this voluptuous vamp than he had initially supposed. He worried that he might potentially disappoint President Ulrich Armstrong, his friend Werther, his father, and all the other accomplices who were bent on exposing Yvette Cartier's willful misdoings.

CHAPTER FOUR

After Werther's hunky, drop-dead gorgeous playmate, Eiden Dreadmiller, had deposited her on the front stoop of her guardians' house, Yvette Cartier sensed, somehow or other, that she had been magically transfigured from the unstable mental condition in which she had found herself only a few short hours agone to a sense of unbounded wholeness and solidity. Prior to going out on this enchanting date with a man whom she now considered serious boyfriend material, she had felt profoundly uncertain about her future, knowing deep down that her present profligate lifestyle was unsustainable and that in time to come there would be an inevasible moment of truth she would have no choice but to meet head-on. Her time spent with Eiden, however, had miraculously lifted this heavy burden of guilt-ridden self-reproach and chronic insecurity from her troubled conscience. The fact that the two of them shared so many of the same moral defects made her feel less unvindicated by her unethical lifestyle, in short: her near-about pathological resistance to all categorical imperatives, especially as regards her questionable practice of hiring complete strangers to do her academic research assignments in her behalf. Whilst immersed in these reflections, an inexplicable tingling sensation ran all through her that she had never experienced before.

Her adoptive mother had been waiting up for her to find out how her date had gone. Of course, as was natural for a young person, Yvette was disinclined to go into too much detail about it, so she relayed to her, with as much of a poker face as she could muster, that her date had been "fair-to-middling."

"Evie," said her adoptive mother, "I have scores of papers to correct in my study tonight, so I'll be going at it quite late, but I just wanted to let you know that your governess has been trying to get ahold of you for a good part of the evening. She said, in no uncertain terms, that she would like to have a short word with you. Are you available to speak with her at the moment?"

"Sure thing, Mummy. I'll ring her up on my landline."

Yvette climbed the three flights of stairs to her bedroom to call back her governess, Prunelda—a stern, taciturn woman for whom she'd never had much of a liking. Prunelda picked up on the first ring, as if anticipating her call.

"Hello, is that you, Evie?"

"Yes ma'am, what can I do for you?" replied Yvette in her over-starchy, custom-tailored-for-Prunelda, passive-aggressive tone of voice.

"I got a message from Helga, Dean Armstrong's wife, earlier this evening. She told me she was anxious to have a word with you in her office tomorrow, as early as possible. Can you let me know a good time that you can meet her so I can schedule it for you in your planner?"

"Did Ms. Armstrong mention what this was regarding?" asked Yvette warily.

"No, Evie. Obviously, your academic work has gone extraordinarily well, so my guess is that it might have something to do with a merit scholarship the school's offering you. I heard some hints dropped through the grapevine about several members of a scholarship subcommittee who are planning to fly in from halfway across the country next week for the sole purpose of bestowing upon you a generous stipend in recognition of the academic excellence of your research. Or something to that effect. Of course, I could be wrong, but Helga sounded unusually bubbly and enthusiastic, as if she had some exciting news to relay to you."

Yvette was skeptical but didn't want to give her governess that impression, so she brightened her tone some and suggested that 2:00 PM the following day would be perfect.

"Okay, thanks Evie. I'll call Helga back right now to let her know."

Allutterly spent to the point of feeling an overwhelming, nearmost stupefying, swell of immoral exhaustion, Yvette fell onto her blanket-fair with a flurry of pent-up emotions welling with a vengeance inside her. It had slowly come to her surrealization, earlier that evening, that, contrary to all expectations, she had, in point of fact, luxuriated in the sensation of being tongued inside her kissing trap by her "ex's" studmeister playmate, Eiden Dreadmiller, and had ne'ertofore surrealized how hard down hot and fabuliciously flaming this scrumptiously vicious, blooded young patrician was.

By no means unakin to the mate cannibalism practiced by female black widow spiders, Yvette had felt an all but uncontrollable tickling inside her to gobble up Eiden's intromittent manhood and swallow it whole. She could still feel herself inwardly atremble from the touch of his cool lunch-hooks as they'd stealthily crept up her thighs into her micro miniskirt. The dinner and conversation had also gone amazingly well, and the food had been positively scrumdiddliumptious! She felt deep within her soul and spirit a newfound confidence that she hadn't been kidding herself but had genuinely enjoyed Eiden's company, for, in comparison with that companion of his she used to date—the pathetic little dweeb Werther Nemesinovich (what a nebbish!)—Eiden knew exactly how to engineer all the right maneuvers to ensure the satisfaction of the all but unsatisfiable young woman she fashioned herself to be, and this made her feel ecstatically proud and happy. And then, to top it all off, this news of a possible scholarship and an easy-peasy, well-paid part-time McJob to placate the powers that be sounded almost too good to be true.

And yet …

And yet … for all that, something vaguely bothered her that she couldn't quite put her finger on. Something that didn't quite tally right. She could not help but wonder why it was that the dean & president's wife Helga, rather than the dean & president himself, had summoned her for a chit-chat in her office, especially if it had anything to do with her academic performance (whether deemed acceptable or not was far from the point). Also, why had Helga contacted her governess Prunelda instead of Prunelda's charge, to wit: *herself?* The luniversity, after all, had Yvette's tardphone and landline numbers in its files. She wondered if, percase, certain parties within the corridors of power were frightened out of their wits at the sight of their own shadows following them whithersoever they chanced to set foot, and that, mayhaps, they perceived our heroine as more of a threat than an asset. But then, what prezactly would persuade them to think in such terms? What fathomable reason could they have to be afraid of *her* of all people? None of these apparently inconsequential, niggling little discrepancies added up (at least from Yvette's perspective). It all seemed kind of askew, not unlike learning asudden that one has been dwelling on the obverse side of a Möbius strip, or something of the sort. These puzzling incongruities caused our heroine to experience a mild case of the heebie-jeebies, which made her thrimble ever so slightly.

Still and all, she figured, there seemed to be little point in losing any sleep over it. 'Twas time to retire to Bedfordshire for a good night's rest, as it had come to be accrescently evident that she had, by the standards of her personal work value-system, a long hard day ahead of her.

THE AT-YOUR-BECK FELICITY CONVEYOR | 29

CHAPTER FIVE

On Thursday morning Mr. Justyce Dreadmiller called a meeting of all his full- and part-time employees. A couple of days prior thereto he had sent out invites to his most loyal patrons, urging them to attend as well. Mildred's Market, which was half the size of an ordinary supermarket, was, in despite of its relatively modest dimensions, commodious enough to serve the needs of the neighboring community. The store offered its patrons a prodigious abundance of high-quality, locally sourced organic produce, ethically slaughtered grass-, legume-, and forb-fed carnivorous fare (which included individual bios and obituaries accompanying each chunk of flesh from harvested livestock), fresh-caught wild fish, and free-range poultry; a deli to die for (modeled after Harrods in London); and all the finest local, gourmet, and upscale goods he could fit on his shelves to ensure the highest attainable standard of guaranteed-or-your-money-back customer satisfaction.

Mr. Dreadmiller was pleased to see that by 9:00 AM all of his sixty-plus full- and part-time employees, together with over a hundred of his most loyal patrons, had shown up for the meeting. At ten minutes past the hour the doors were deadbolted shut and signs were taped to the windows, as well as on sandwich boards installed at the various means of egress, with messages scrawled upon them communicating the profoundest of apologies from the management to customers for any inconveniences caused by the market's temporary closure and notifying them withal that it would be re-opened at the crack of noon. Although he had rented 150 folding chairs for this special event, many of those who attended preferred standing in the aisles, which was perfectly fine from his point of view. When everyone was settled in place, he cleared his throat and commenced his semi-rehearsed speech.

"Ladies and gentlemen, I want to thank all of you so much for showing up here this morning on relatively short notice. I would also like to express to you, my dear employees, my deepest appreciation for your steadfast loyalty, your unflinching honesty, and your dedicated hard work. You are like an extended family to me and I want you to know that I value and love each and every one of you as my own. I am confident, beyond measure, that I can always depend on you in times of need and, reciprocally, I want you to know, beyond any niggling doubts you might harbor, that I am fairly and morally beholden to each and every one of you and shall likewise, within my professional purview, always be there to lend you a helping hand if and whensoever the need should present itself."

Justyce Dreadmiller took a moment to scan his audience, the preponderant majority of whose members appeared to be alert and attentive and who, en bloc, exuded a positive, sympathetic vibe. Upcheered thereby, he expectorated a worm of nasal mucus into a muck-rag and went on with his morale-boosting pep talk, "I see that many of my most loyal patrons have shown up today, for which I also wish to express my heartfelt and humble gratitude. Please know that the fact you are here this morning means the world to me!" He withdrew a lachrymatory from his breast pocket to wipe away the cornball tear-blobs that had started freely flowing from his momentanely mushy nebshaft, whereupon he made the swiftest of all comebacks.

"Well, I'll cut right to the chase then," he said. "We have been compelled, of late, to come to grips with an unresolved concern hereabouts in connection with an enticingly attractive young prodigy with sticky fingers who is everly on the filch and exhibits a personal preference, 'twould seem, for operating off her own bat. This coquettish young croshabelle—a piece of toothsome eye candy, to be sure— has proven herself to be prolific in a host of singular gifts and talents and has, consequentially, continued to return to our humble mom-and-pop shop on a quasi quotidian basis for the past two and a half years. Her modus operandi is to rap and rend our highest priced feminine articles from the pharmaceutical section of the grocery—little girly type things like cosmetics, perfumes, sex oils and whatnot. This ceaseless snaveling of articles off our shelves has caused a cumulative loss in dispendious merchandise valued at upwards of $90,000.00 at the wholesale price and well over $150,000.00 at its estimated retail value."

Mr. Dreadmiller paused to allow his audience to absorb this shocking disclosure of information and was overjoyed to witness a loud and spontaneous ignition of violent verbal flare-ups and fulminations (accompanied by a sea of upraised fists, clenched for combat) from a receptive, simpatico audience whose members were keenly bent on expressing their righteous disgust and moral outrage with wrath- ful "ooo's & ah's" intermingled with whoops and hollers of: "Wicked li'l beezie!" "Goodness bodacious!" "Call in the cavalry!" "Scone her on the dot!" "Sly li'l sloot, ain't she?" "Ought be branded with yer shop's logo on her bare bombosity, mon- sieur—*at strict minimum!*" "Fie fer shame!" "String her assways on a roulette wheel an' spin her like a fidget!" "Make her fang what she swoops!" "Show her who's boss, Herr Dreadmiller!" "Revamp her modus vivendi!" "Give her a good dose of Doctor Greenwade's medicine, *and then some,* sir!" "Take her to the woodshed for a long hard health check!" "Tan her tushy!" "Learn her a stout refresher course in the pre- cepts & principles of proper etiquette!" "Twank her!" "Rectify her moral compass!" "Dangle her in the meat section!" and similar such calls for condign valentines— crescendoing to a climax of murtherous indignation that thundered from every quarter of the commercial space in which they were assembled. It was immensely reassuring to Mr. Dreadmiller to know that these were upstanding, hard-working, high-principled, law-abiding citizens—paragons of virtue, the very pillars of society, the ultimate embodiments of perfection in their chosen fields of expertise—who stood one thousand percent behind him and then some.

Mr. Dreadmiller cleared his throat and went on with his zealous monopologue. "These nearabout systematic unchastised thefts have, disventurously for ye, my dear employees, precluded my having in possession suffisant wherewithal to raise thy salaries, as I've been longing to do for the past couple years, for which I meekly beg thy forgiveness (and forbearance), for I have devised a plan to see this encumbrance to our forward movement duly rectified within the foreseeable future and have thus invited all of ye here today in the hopes that I can prevail upon ye to volunteer thine expert hands in implementing the various and sundry procedural facilitations necessitated for the felicitous technical execution of this prodigiously daunting endeavor, as I am confident that each and every one of ye has a substantial vested interest in helping all of those foregathered here this primetide to do whatsoever is necessary, even if it means 'getting blood from a turnip,' as they say, to achieve this noble and dearworthy objective."

There was an ultroneous chicken fit of applause from all quarters, which dissipated into a quack, whereupon Mr. Dreadmiller forged ahead with his persuasive cordiloquy.

"As many of ye have undoubtedly got wind of, we're about to have this thrilling new belt conveying contraption installed inside our store, come blue o'clock on the morrow. It's nothing like the mundane checkout counter belts to which the predominant share of ordinary, average citizens has grown complacently acclimated over the years. Nor is it anything on par with the unsightly meat belt conveyors that (what with all their breakages, mistrackings, hygienic risks, and so on) are apt to being operated behind the scenes in a good many fish markets and butcheries. This modern apparatus was designed, developed, and manufactured by leading engineers, trailblazing technologists, and percipient government-employed facilitators in Japan. And the Japanese, unlike most of us Genericans (as ye may concur or beg to differ as thou wilt), have an amazing knack for being attentive to what might seem to average Joe-lunchbucket & Billy-sixpack types (like yours truly)"—Mr. Dreadmiller paused with a self-defecating dopey grin on his phizog accompanied by a nudge-nudge, wink-wink, which drew hail-fellow-well-met cackles, snorts, and rah-rahs from two or three illustrious afilliates of the old boy/girl network in the audience—"to be the most picayune details, which is one reason they are renowned for their creative technological innovations. Many of ye in the know have already witnessed the amazing tricks the forementioned appliance is capable of performing when its thousand-and-one nifty accessories are pressed into service. I am fully confident that once this device is successfully installed, it will contribute immensely to a shopping experience bordering on the sublime for each and every one of ye, my dear and worthy patrons!" The grocer made a broad gesticulation of salutation with both of his arms towards those parties in the audience he was addressing, maintaining pointed eye contact with several of the people he either knew or recognized.

"And a work experience that will feel more akin to a recreational adventure for all of ye, my treasured employees!" He blew exaggerated kisses of affection to the members of his staff.

"I have, confessedly, felt a bit ambivalent about getting law enforcement involved in the matter of dealing with this inveterate booster, as I think we can straighten things out far more effectively, and to our greatest possible advantage, by making the very best use of our own personal resources—which, I might add, are vast beyond measure!" He raised both of his arms once again to make a sweeping all-inclusive gesture of felicitation & benediction, as well as to agnize the indestructible bonds of universal harmony, peace, and brotherly/sisterly love and good will that united them in their just cause, after which there followed a brief round of appreciative applause as a natural response to hearing the ebullient grocer singing the highest praises of all parties in attendance.

"The individual members of my immediate nuclear family," continued Mr. Dreadmiller, "each and every one of whom possesses their own unique sets of talents and capabilities, have been hyper-enthusiastically supportive of the plans I have devised for achieving our objectives, and many faculty members from the local schools are contributing their knowledge and expertise to this by-no-stretch unambitious undertaking. Morefurther, we have on our side Professor Ulrich Armstrong, who, as many of you know, has earnt a distinguished reputation for administrating Pimpleton State Luniversity, as both its dean and president, with (if you pardon the time-worn cliché) 'an iron fist in a velvet glove'—but don't let yourselves be fooled by such mealy-mouthed euphemisms, folks, namely: by the soft, silky, sumptuous associations you may nourish in your minds & souls with reference to the smooth woven fabric we all know and love as 'velvet,' for Professor Armstrong is one helluva tough cookie, or what's better known in the vernacular as a 'mean-ass mothafucka.' Indeed, 'twould be far more exaccurate to say he administrates the school 'with a tungsten morning star in a mitt of molten lead!'— and who accordingly has full access to all the most invaluable resources from the luniversity in terms of its discretionary funding (accrued over the years from an impressive roster of billion & trillionaire donors) and personnel, including many renowned & distinguished faculty members and, last but not least, his beautiful and enterprising young wife, Helga, who has agreed to assist us in this ultra complex, cross-functional, multi-dimensional enterprise.

"I have already made the downpayment on the conveyor belt apparatus, which, as per indicated, is due to be delivered and installed here at the crack of dawn *mañana*. We should be able to keep the store open during regular business hours tomorrow whilst six or seven dozen electrical, mechanical, biomedical, computer, and nano-technology engineers, who've been flown in on chartered flights from Osaka and Tokyo, perform and finalize the Felicity Conveyor's installation. Once everything is properly in place, the device will be tested to make sure it's fully operational, and then, in exactly a week from now, at 1:00 PM next Thursday, we are scheduled to have an inauguration ceremony and fundraiser, to which everyone here and abroad is invited, during which time a dazzling array of refreshments will be served by professional caterers from our spirit shop and deli.

"And so, without further ado, I shall have my son Eiden and my daughter Celine pass out the classified instruction booklets, fresh from the printers, that outline our precise plans of execution for the purpose of rectifying irrevocably the aforecited matter."

Mr. Dreadmiller went on for the next two-and-a-half hours to delineate his strategies in meticulous detail, with occasional short lectures delivered by key luniversity faculty members, whereupon at noon sharp the store re-opened and everybody, excepting the employees with day shifts, departed with their individual assignments in hand.

CHAPTER SIX

Y vette showed up promptly at 2:00 PM Thursday afternoon to meet with Helga, the dean & president's wife, at her beautifully appointed office overlooking the campus quad. Helga was seated in a Pininfarina Xten Ergonomic Chair behind a hand-crafted spiral mahogany executive desk from Italy that had cherry veneers with walnut, rosewood, and ebony inlays. Hanging on the wall was a grandiose oversize professional photo portrait of a stunningly attractive, albeit severe looking, young blonde woman whom Yvette all but took as given to be Helga & Ulrich Armstrong's eldest daughter, and who looked to be roughly Yvette's age. The young woman's eyes appeared (at least from Yvette's vantage point) to follow her around the room, irrespective of where she was situated, which our subdebutante found not a trife unsettling, even a mite bit creepy (if that's the proper term to account for the shuddery sensations it produced all over her body). This provocative—dare it be said, "in-your-face"—photo was not unlikenable to a feminized version of "Big Brother is Watching You!"

She felt a touch of skepticism as to whether this appointment with Ms. Armstrong had anything to do with an offer of a merit scholarship, as intimated by her governess Prunelda, as she knew in her heart of hearts that she had proved herself time and again to be an astonishingly unexceptional, if not arrantly sub-mediocre, student, notwithstanding the outward appearance of a perfect GPA in her transcripts. And it was by no means unlikely that a good many of her professors suspected as much, especially in light of how little she participated in classroom discussions. She sensed it was an ingrained habit of her teachers to studiously "look the other way" for the purpose of avoiding unnecessary conflicts, or potentially ugly confrontations, with their students (herself not discluded), for fear that they would receive scathingly contemptuous reviews from them, for it was unqualifiedly paramount, from their own perspectives, not to draw the unwanted attention of their higher-echelon colleagues, especially if they were still in the academic limbo of holding on for dear life to cliffhanging tenure-track positions. They were, most of them, extremely busy all the time to the point of having transmogrified over the years from seeming self-assured young upstarts into overwrought, bug-eyed nervous wrecks, many of whom had developed violent, albeit perfectly idiosyncratic, facial tics (that is to say, sudden and uncontrollable jerkings of their heads accompanied by external grimaces, spasmodic movements of their tongues, involuntary nictations and palpebrations of their orbits, among other things) as well as vocal tics that included barking, grunting, snorting, sniffing, and tongue clicking in conjunction with the utterances of foul expletives and unparliamentary profanities, the latter pair of which quirks she assumed to be outward manifestations of a neurological disorder known as Tourette's Syndrome.

It was not surprising, then, that these low-level faculty members would evince a pronounced penchant for prioritizing their own research interests over the interests of their students and that they were, for that reason, markedly hesitant to ruffle any feathers that might lead to their being perceived by the powers in office as belonging to a distinctive breed of maladjusted individuals who possessed a singular predilection for alienating their upper-echelon colleagues—namely: those who held them in a virtual life-or-death grip. If these low-level faculty members had been appreciably higher on the academic food chain, such disagreements, especially challenges made to those who were at an even higher level in this factitious hierarchical structure, then in all likelihood it would take little more than a backhanded compliment (or even something as seemingly minuscule as a micro-second's hesitation in response to a loaded question that might readily be misinterpreted as a calculated personal slight) to cause all this pent-up passive-aggressive energy to explode into the most vicious imaginable infighting over internal allocations of limited funding for this or that (especially as it pertained to the financial needs of special-interest groups in various departments throughout the luniversity).

Yvette well knew, from having listened to her guardians' horror stories at the dinner table, how brutal and bloodthirsty such infighting among faculty could become, even, at times, verging on physical violence that could lead to broken bones, fractured skulls, or even (God forbid!) a missing eye. Paradoxically, all of these professorial feuds and squabbles may well have been to our subdebutante's strategic advantage insofar as assuring that she would remain effectively safeguarded from being disciplined with penalties ranging from mere slaps on the wrist to permanent expulsion from the academy. This was a result of the deeply entrenched system of checks and balances that remained firmly in place (not unlike the barbed wire enclosures one sees in zoological gardens for desperate, dangerous, and destructive animalian creatures for the purpose of keeping them at bay from unsanctioned meals) between the low-, middle-, and high-ranking brass on the luniversity teaching & administrative faculties, the overwhelming preponderance of whose affiliates were kept in near constant preoccupation with either securing their positions aboard what they rightly or wrongly hypothesized to be a seafaring vessel of sorts, even if they were only hanging from the gangplank edges thereof by the skins of their teeth, or by seeking whatsoever means were necessary (all ethics & morals be damned!) to throw their perceived rivals, competitors, and adversaries overboard in premeditatedly sabotaged personal floatation devices to ensure they would sink and eventually drown in the turbulent waters besieging their stricken ship from all sides.

This having been said, it was no big deal, then, for Yvette Cartier to hire ghost-writers and to pay them exorbitant online fees for their essay writing services, as no one on the luniversity faculty had the time or energy to give so much as a flying fig, one way or the other, how she went about polishing off her class assignments. Because of her Great Uncle Weaser's unbounded generosity, she was able to have her own private PayPal account that enabled her to purchase whatever online services she happened to crave (both academic and nonacademic alike). The faculty at Pimpleton State knew that her guardians were relatively high-ranking professors at the school and that, over and above that, her guardians made no bones about leveraging their powerful political influence to crush anybody they perceived as having wronged or slighted them in any way whatsoever—that is, if they felt a strong compulsion to do so—not only within but also well beyond the confines of the Pimpleton State Luniversity campus. The fact that virtually every party occupying a position at Pimpleton State trembled with fear and trepidation in the presence of her adoptive parents put our Spoilt Highness in an exceptionally advantageous position as a student at said institution, seeing as none of her professors had any desire whatsoever to cross swords with her guardians, knowing it could potentially handicap their careers if they durst to do so. Long story short: Mademoiselle Cartier was untouchable.

"So, Yvette," said Helga Armstrong, taking her in with piercing orbits that seemed to cut right through her soul, "how are your classes going at school?"

"Um … fine. I'm enjoying them very much," she answered, trying to sound as upbeat as possible.

"That's good to hear," said Helga. "The reason I asked you to come here today is that I heard through the grapevine that you were looking for a part-time job to help supplement your income and thereby mitigate the burden of your tuition and living expenses."

"Uh … yeah, that's right. Who told you about that?"

"A lovely young lady named Celine Dreadmiller, who notified us that you're a close friend of her brother's."

Yvette was surprised that this news had circulated so rapidly, as she had received the phone call from Prunelda about scheduling today's meeting at the very instant she had arrived home last night. It seemed at the time that Prunelda had already been anxiously awaiting her return for several hours to relay the message appertaining to this purportedly "urgent" appointment with Ms. Armstrong. The timing didn't quite make sense, for it would mean that Eiden would have had to have made several phone calls in a manner of mere seconds after depositing her on the front stoop of her guardians' home the night before. Although Yvette was suspicious that something conspiratorial was afoot, she was nevertheless more inclined to attribute such discrepancies to being mere coincidences or, perhaps, "meaningful coincidences" or "synchronicities," or what Carl Jung defined as "acausal connecting principles." In such situations it is possible that psychological events, such as

Yvette's deep heartfelt emotions after spending time with Eiden the night before, were linked in some fashion to external world events that might objectively seem meaningfully related, notwithstanding that they wouldn't have any discernible causal connection. In other words, it was most probably nothing she ought to feel all that concerned about.

"Indeed," said Yvette, "Eiden told me all about his sister. I would love to meet her some day."

Helga Armstrong pressed a red button on her desk that made a strident buzzing noise just outside her door, whereupon, almost instantaneously, a beautiful young woman in ultra chic, luxury-brand designer clothes glissaded into Helga's office outstretching her right hand towards Yvette.

"Celine Dreadmiller. Very pleased to meet you," she said whilst snatching Yvette's semi-proffered hand and squeezing it firmly.

Yvette's complexion became suffused with a deep rosy blush, for she couldn't believe that things were moving along so quickly and, again, for the life of her, was unable to account for this uncanny quinkydink. "Likewise," answered Yvette with a smile that was half fake and half genuine. "Your brother told me all about you—all good things, of course. I'm very pleased to meet you as well."

"Okay, girls," said Helga, rising from her desk, "I have another appointment in a couple minutes. Ms. Cartier, Celine will drive you to the cosmetics and love toy warehouse so you can become acquainted with the spot where you're scheduled to start working tomorrow. I'm glad you finally found the chance to meet one another after all these years, seeing as the two of you share so much in common. Sartorially speaking, especially. Come what may, I have the utmost confidence that you'll get along famously and find each other's company singularly—how should I put it?—rewarding. Take good care of yourselves, both of you! Have a wonderful day!"

As Celine and Yvette strolled towards Celine's Pagani Zonda HP Barchetta supercar (in actuality it had been lent her for the day by one of her famous fashionista friends), Yvette observed that Celine was more than a foot taller than she was and looked to be approximately five to six years her senior. This lent to her a hyper-competitive, superior-at-all-costs edge, and also afforded her an impressively commanding and imperious demeanor. She felt Celine's talons pinching her right elbow from behind, almost as if she were being detained for questioning by a rule-bound officer of the law.

When they arrived at Celine's car, which was parked in a private garage on campus, she gave Yvette a little nudge from behind and said, "Get in! We'll take my whip for a little spin before I drive you to the warehouse where you'll start working tomorrow. This way the two of us can become better acquainted."

Celine drove like a speed demon all around the city, making swift razor-sharp turns around blind corners with only a single palm on the steering wheel. Her driving rattled Yvette's already unsteadied nerves. At one point our heroine caught herself reaching for an imaginary barf bag in the glove compartment.

"So," said Celine, turning her head towards Yvette, with her eyes off the road, "I heard you, like, had this little thing going with my brother last night. Pardon me if I seem a bit intrusive, but I'm curious to know how you feel about him. Do you think this is looking to be, like, a long-term relationship or something?"

The bluntness and audacity of Celine's query caught our heroine completely off guard.

"He seems nice," she replied noncommittally, whilst gripping the panic bar on the passenger door. Realizing after a moment that she hadn't really satisfactorily answered Celine's invasive query, she attempted in her mind to formulate a response that would be acceptable without giving away her true feelings about Eiden. Before she even had a chance, however, to respond, or was able to gain a purchase upon what was happening all around her, Celine Dreadmiller whisked her cruiser into a private downtown parking facility and opened the passenger door to let her subject out. Once again, Celine pinched Yvette by her elbow from behind and led her down a stairwell into a cavernous warehouse that was chock-full of boxes of designer cosmetics, fancy exotic perfumes, little jars of sex odors, high-end arousal lubes, vibrators of various shapes and sizes, and other similar such things. It made Yvette feel like a chocoholic child in a chocolate factory.

"The facilities," said Celine, "include a desk with a telephone where all you have to do is pick up to answer calls and take messages. Truthfully, there are usually no more than one or two calls per day and on many days none whatsoever. There's also a nicely appointed kitchen, well-stocked with comestibles which are re-supplied within the hour on request, a comfortable bedroom with a high-tech entertainment center, a modern bathroom with a Toto Neorest NX2 Dual Flush Toilet with Actilight and a high-end luxury designer shower unit.

"I swing by once or twice a week, usually in the early evening hours, to retrieve my messages, if there are any. The pay we offer is $666.00 per hour and the work shifts are in five-hour increments for only four days a week: Tuesdays through Fridays from 12:00 noon to 5:00 PM. You'll be provided a key to the premises and are welcome to stay here and make yourself perfectly at home whenever you like. In fact, you're more than welcome to spend nights here if it suits your needs. Please feel free to think of this space as your very own private living quarters. Any questions...?"

Yvette had a list of questions in her mind but didn't wish to offend her new boss, so she simply replied, "No, ma'am. I think everything's perfectly clear. It sounds like a spectacular job!"

"Very well then, just sign this contract on the dotted line and we'll be all set. I'll bring you the keys to your new digs tomorrow, right here in front of the warehouse, at noon sharp."

CHAPTER SEVEN

Seated comfortably in her private office on campus, Helga Armstrong dialed the contact number Prunelda had provided her. It was a phone number Prunelda had found in Yvette's bedroom in a small dog-eared old diary hidden underneath her mattress. Now that Yvette had a day job of sorts and was away from home at predictable hours, Prunelda was able to perform some of the reconnaissance errands that had been assigned her by Justyce Dreadmiller and his task force during the Thursday morning meeting at Mildred's Market. She had found a suspicious looking motto scrawled at the bottom corner of one of the pages in the diary that was directly adjacent to a phone number circled in red ink: "You pull the caper, we write the paper!" When she entered the motto in a search engine online it was instantaneously connected to a discreet essay writing company owned by a gentlemen called Dweebaldo Van Boofus, who had a PhD honorific affixed to his nomenclature, apparently to lend his services a mark of credibility. Prunelda had figured he must have been a disgruntled old graduate who had failed to find a teaching position and did this kind of unethical hackwork for a living in lieu of the real deal. It made perfect sense, as it was, quite possibly, one of the best ways he could exact his revenge against the system that had failed him so miserably.

A crusty, groggy sounding middle-aged male voice answered on the first ring.

"And...?"

"Hello, is this Dr. Dweebaldo Van Boofus?"

"One and the same. And *you* are...?"

"My name's Helga Armstrong. I'm the acting assistant to Professor Ulrich Armstrong, who, as you may know, is president and dean of Pimpleton State Luniversity. May I have a moment of your time, sir?"

Dweebaldo Van Boofus cleared his throat. "Why certainly, Ms. Armstrong. I must say, this is a bolt from the blue. How can I be of service?"

"I would like to propose a gig for you and promise I will do my utmost to make it very much worth your while."

"I'm all ears, Ms. Armstrong!" replied Dweebaldo.

After explaining in some detail what was being requested of him and then receiving an immediate response from him in the emphatic affirmative, accentuated with what sounded like a dollop of mustard, Helga asked the disaffected ghostwriter to come over to her office at his "earliest possible convenience" (which was a genteelism for "straightaway") to sign a contract that included a clause of the strictest confidentiality, which was, for all intents and purposes, tantamount to a "top secret" government classification. With an implied threat of possible reprisals were he to be caught, or even so much as vaguely suspected of, leaking the eentsy-weentsiest niffnaff of information, blowing so much as even the tiddlywinkiest of all dog whistles, or in any other way betraying confidences by letting his lips run loose without a leash (whether intended or no), she made him swear on his mother's grave not to mention any details of this conversation to anybody—not even to his pet snake or goldfish. Dweebaldo Van Boofus reassured her that he understood everything with perfect clarity and that he would keep his lips tightly sealed even if it meant nailing them shut with deadbolts. "Not to worry, ma'am!" he said. "Mum's the word!"

Upon replacing the receiver, it felt to Dr. Van Boofus as though he had just been hired by a secret government agency to do its dirty work off the radar. He didn't much mind this, however, as he could certainly use the money.

CHAPTER EIGHT

"See, I told you it would be a cushy job, didn't I?" said Eiden as he sat on the crocodile leather futon with his arm around Yvette. For the past several days the two of them had become an item. He had ascertained that the reason Yvette had an irrepressible penchant for wearing seductively short micro miniskirts (sans unmentionables) was that she loved being spanked on her bare bottom and sexually humiliated by stern authoritative men, something that Eiden had intuited on first meeting her. He figured that this kink of hers was most likely the fundamental reason the relationship hadn't worked out so well between Yvette and his buddy Werther, notwithstanding that Eiden knew for a fact, from many frank and lengthy discussions with his dear friend, that Werther was, forsooth, a maniacally vicious, savagely brutal sexual sadist who operated at the most extreme ends of the BDSM spectrum. Werther Nemesinovich absolutely deliciated in the merciless infliction of excruciating pain—that is to say, legit no-joke pain, Pain with a capital P, pain that really hurt—on the backsides of reverential female scapegoats who themselves got a psychoemotional charge out of being on the receiving end of his cruel valentines. Of course, this was always consensual, albeit in the sense of being a kind of consensual non-consensuality (on steroids, if thou wilt) on the part of his devoted victims, who were usually sweet & petite, mim-mouthed, meeverly, milk-faced young women who apparently derived untold pleasure at experiencing intolerable pain on their quivering, nubile young anatomies or, at very least, had been systematically brainwashed (read: mind-raped) by the algolagnic subculture wherewith they were affiliated into featuring that they felt a liquorish oblectation at being ferociously flogged, even to the point where they would insist upon remunerating Werther with exorbitant monthly retainers for his on-call punishment services (and furtherover, they were always more than happy to leave him handsome gratuities into the bargain) without actually realizing that, by the same token, Werther himself would have been pleased as punch to compensate these young ladies (and by no means ungenerously) for the honor and privilege of being given carte blanche to torment and humiliate them through the lens of his highly innovative disciplinal methodologies. Aside from the intense pleasure it gave his victims, it also purified their souls in the sense of expiating them of their else-ways (what they believed to be) unforgivable sins and transgressions.

Werther belonged to various pain-lovers' clubs and performance art movements with experimental practices that were so far out on the fringes (some of which were in part energized by the toxic influence of Hermann Nitsch and the Viennese Actionism movement of the late 20th century), that certain of their artist members did unorthodox things to their bodies such as nailing themselves to Volkswagen Beetles (in emulation of the late American artist Christopher Lee Burden) and other higher-end car brands such as BMWs, cutting off their earlobes (à la the contemporary Russian artist Petr Pavlensky), or, in some cases amputating their partner's limbs and/or cutting off their own organs of reproduction (the latter of which was inspired by Japanese artist Mao Sugiyama's "Testicle Banquet," a performance art piece in which the artist underwent elective genital-removal surgery and then allowed his severed penis, testicles, and scrotal skin, seasoned with parsley and garnished with mushrooms, to be served to guests at an upscale dinner party).

Werther Nemesinovich, who most adolescent schoolgirls (that is to say, those in his immediate orbit, including Yvette) had regarded as a weird & unbalanced creepazoid from outer space when he was a student at the Pimpleton Heights Prep Academy, confided to Eiden that he adored the sound of beautiful submissive young women begging him for mercy as he drew deep welts on their backsides and fronts with the cracks and swirls of canes, switches, paddles, riding crops, cattle goads, bullwhips, and all the rest. Notwithstanding Werther's constitutional proclivity for unbridled sexual sadism, Eiden knew him, on all other levels, to be a consummately sweet, shy, gentle, sensitive, soft-spoken, and eminently likeable young man, with the remnants of a baby face, who treated everyone—especially women of all shapes, forms, and sizes—with the utmost kindness, compassion, empathy, dignity, and respect. The problem Werther had encountered in his short-lived relationship with Yvette was that she had never given him so much as a snowflake's chance in the lowest circle of the Inferno to show her the magnificent collection of skeletons he kept hidden from his mother under a trapdoor inside his closet, which lack of disclosure had the detrimental effect of boring Yvette to tears to the point where she had esteemed it incumbent upon herself, in her own best interests, to give Eiden's buddy the old heave-ho. Although she cared not a whit that he had fallen desperately in love with her, Yvette considered the twelve-thousand-dollar Blue Nile diamond stud earrings from Tiffany's as a well-earned gratuity for her having given Werther the time of day and thus had no qualms whatsoever about hanging on to them, not as a keepsake per se (God forbid, as the memories of time spent in Werther's company meant absolutely nothing to her) but rather as a portfolio investment in speculation of its potential accrual in value as a property asset over time. Ah, thought Eiden, but if only she had caught but a fleeting glimpse (howsoever infinitesimal it may have been at the time) of Werther's true colors...!

If only...!

Eiden, who was only a few months older than Yvette, did his utmost best to fulfill the role she desired of him, which worked out extraordinarily well for both parties, as he loved playing the dominant role in their relationship, a role on his part that she seemed so desperately to crave. He surmised that this submissive propensity of hers could very well have been due to her having, at the present moment, a male guardian who was so caught up in his academic research in dialectical hermeneutics, that he had in all probability spent very little one-on-one time with his adoptive teenage daughter. Thus, he surmised (quite correctly) that Yvette craved fatherly attention, even if it meant being spanked by him all day and all night for her gratuitously unforgivable transgressions. Both Eiden and Yvette worked out a routine together wherethrough they played out their sexual fantasies and desires. She would recurrently steal cosmetics and sex toys from the warehouse adjoining her apartment and he would role-play by pretending to be the owner who discovered her thievish malefactions. He would then scold her harshly, citing the Seventh Commandment, "Thou shalt not steal," and quoting other pertinent scriptures, such as Proverbs, chapter 10, verse 2, "Treasures of wickedness profit nothing: But righteousness delivereth from death," Ephesians, chapter 4, verse 28, "Let him that stole steal no more: but rather let him labor, working with his hands the thing which is good, that he may have to give to him that needeth," and, more forebodingly, Exodus, chapter 22, verse 7, "If a man shall deliver unto his neighbor money or stuff to keep, and it be stolen out of the man's house; if the thief be found, let him pay double." He would then summarily order her to strip completely naked in a tone of voice that brooked no argument, whereto she would haltingly submit with feigned reluctance. In a nutshell, our subdebutante would comply, howsoever grudgingly, to each and every one of his stern and authoritative-sounding commands, no matter how unsavory, off-putting, or objectionable she adjudged them to be, and, moreover, she would pointedly assume a petulantly pouty look of wary yet wanton anticipation on her dial. He would then order her to lie completely still whilst he spanked her firmly on her vulnerably exposed and duly elevated posteriors, always with the threat that he would strap her down by her wrists and ankles, and even invite his friends over for a look-see, if she failed to quit her incessant fidgeting (which, he could not help but note, appeared to be an inborn tendency of hers). The futon in her luxury digs was made of a smooth, soft crocodile leather that was cool to the touch, which greatly enhanced her pleasure at being punished in this fashion.

At this point in their relationship Eiden feared he was fast becoming smitten with Yvette and that there would be no turning back. Or so he believed *ab initio*, whilst lost in the throes of what can only fitly be described as an uncontainable carnal obsession.

CHAPTER NINE

"I appreciate your going out of the way for us on such short notice, Dr. Van Boofus," said Helga Armstrong, seated at her desk with a picturesque view of the campus quad that could be taken in through the arched windows directly behind her.

"Your offer is well-nigh impossible for me to refuse, ma'am," replied the aggrieved ghostwriter.

"So, just to make sure we're singing the same tune," she said, "the deadline for Mademoiselle Cartier's upcoming research paper is for 8:00 AM Friday next week in Professor Xeroxburger's Astrophysiology class. Is that correct, Dr. Van Boofus?"

"You got it!" he replied.

"And I want to make sure that you fully comprehend what we are asking you to do and what the possible risks are to your reputation for discretion amongst your clients."

"I absolutely do, Ms. Armstrong!"

"Very well then." She handed Dr. Van Boofus a Montblanc solid gold fountain pen and a page of sheepskin parchment. "Please read and sign this contract on the dotted line. You'll receive half of your fee now and the other half when the job's completed. Do you have any questions?"

"No ma'am, none that I can think of. I just want you and your husband to know that I feel profoundly privileged and honored that you have entrusted me with this noble task. I cannot emphasize to you enough what an inestimable blessing it is for me to be asked to serve, in mine own modest capacity as a professional has-been, flameout, and deadbeat (if only as the merest cog in the most negligible wheel of this mightily complex and powerful operation) towards bringing to the fullest possible fruition the glorious denouement of this just and worthy enterprise—all relevant technical, mechanical, and structural details of which you, Ms. Armstrong, have so eloquently outlined for mine 'umble sake. I want to express to you once again my devout and reverent thankfulness for this golden opportunity to serve the exigent needs of our stately community!"

Dr. Van Boofus dropped a deep curtsy upon making his exit from Ms. Armstrong's office, gently shutting the door behind him. Enwrapped in thought, he descended the service stairwell of the campus administration building with a strong, clear, and purposeful sense of the mission he had just been delegated to accomplish. By the time he was crossing the campus quad towards the street where he had parked his vehicle, he felt psychologically empowered to take the bull by the horns.

CHAPTER TEN

"Eiden," said Yvette to her lover, "I'll be out in a few. Thanks in advance for your patience … and forbearance!"

"No problem, sweetheart. Take your time!" answered Eiden with a contented grin on his kissably handsome phizog.

One thing Yvette adored about her new lover was his gentle, easygoing manner coupled with his firm, unwavering hand whenever he tied her up and spanked her on her quivering behind for being such a naughty spoilt little bitch. Even if she kept him waiting for an hour or two, he wouldn't utter a peep of protest but would wait, seeming with the patience of a sniper, for her to step out of the shower in her birthday suit so they could make passionate love on the fancy leather futon in her bedroom.

Yvette entered the palatially appointed bathroom and removed all of her dispendious designer gear, including the flossy diaphanous unwhisperables that payed silent homage to the abstract concept of "lingerie," which she tossed insouciantly over the La Grande Muraglia armchair in her bedroom before stepping into her luxurious shower unit for a quick little sprinkle.

Over the past few days she had grown comfortably acclimated to her new job and all its perks, including the plush accommodations and free access to expensive designer cosmetics, amorous lubricants, pleasure toys, and all the rest. Eiden had reassured her that his sister Celine wouldn't mind her "borrowing" a few items from the adjoining warehouse. He even informed his little wonder-wench that it was one of the sanctioned perquisites of her employment insofar as there was a subtextual implication in the contract she had signed (which she hadn't even bothered reading) that she was expected to have a first-hand knowledge of the products being sold by Celine's company. Of course, in her case that wouldn't be a problem, as she considered herself to be an eminently qualified expert in such matters.

The first couple of days on the job Yvette had been prudently circumspect as to the number of items she appropriated from the shelves of the warehouse, but by the fourth, and especially by the fifth, day, she had virtually thrown all care out the window and become irresponsibly cavalier as to the countless scores of items she purloined, not even bothering to keep track of them any longer. She must have opened hundreds, if not thousands, of boxes containing bottles of exotic perfumes, jars of sex lubricants, imported off-the-wall love toys, aphrodisiacs, sex odors, dildos of varying shapes, sizes, and textures (i.e., silicone, rubber, metal, plastic, and even break-resistant glass), butt plugs for novices and professionals alike, Kegel balls, fanny nudgers, vibrators of every imaginable sort (to wit: double-sided wand vibrators, hands-free vibrators, wearable vibrators, pulse and suction vibrators, ribbed internal vibrators, remote-control bullet vibrators, et cetera), dicks-on-sticks, battery-operated enema bulb syringes, G-spot stimulators, rectal thermometers, nipple clamps, anal beads, and so forth and so on. Yvette would sniff these items, inhale them, spray them on her lady parts, stick them up her bunghole, rub them all over her body, suck on them, insert them in her ears, or just lie completely still and let them do their magic. Before and after business hours, when no one was around, Yvette had (as if making up for lost time) become one of the world's most prolific masturbators, fingering herself in every conceivable way, exploring every hole, crack, and fold of her flesh after lubricating herself with various creams, gels, lotions, and oils. She got so much exercise from hours and hours of masturbating, she never had to worry about dieting or going to the gym. It enhanced her natural beauty and gave her an alluring, almost sirenic, afterglow. Gentlemen from all walks of life would ogle our subdebutante everywhither she set her pretty young feet and, to boost her libidinal ego, she would play little games with these poor sitting ducks by coyly making goo-goo eyes at the throbbing love muscles inside their trousers with the object of egging them on into kidding themselves that they had more than a snowball's chance in perdition of jumping her bones, and then, at the very whip-stitch of an instant at which she arrested their amorous attention, she would avert their concupiscent sidelong looks, feigning a high & mighty Olympian aloofness—a toyous time-tested tactic that would invariably drive her wannabe suitors batshit crazy and leave them in the lurch with ungovernable boners.

It felt incredibly liberating to live and thrive independently, away from her guardians for once—and especially away from her nosy governess Prunelda, whose oppressive companionship she had always found difficult to stomach. Her guardians, on the other hand, had always been permissive by nature. They were most of the time compulsively preoccupied with their academic research, not to mention teaching a buttload of graduate and undergraduate courses at the luniversity. Yvette rarely saw them at home and was actually more likely to run into them on campus between classes. Sometimes it seemed as though they didn't really care all that much where she went, with whom she hung out, or how she spent her spare time. Unlike Prunelda, they were never prying or snoopy and generally avoided asking her uncomfortable questions about her schoolwork and love life. On the other hand, it surprised her unpleasantly that they hadn't bothered to voice any strenuous (much less half-hearted) objections to her moving out of their house into her new digs on such short notice, nor did they seem to mind all that much that her hot-off-the-fire McJob was exceptionally unchallenging. Quite understandably, such a grievance might seem perversely counter-intuitive to the casual observer, for it had long been an article of faith (a foregone conclusion or even an unwritten universal law, if thou wilt), in the current sociocultural milieu, that any college undergraduate student in possession of his or her wits would crave nothing less than to establish (if only incrementally) a sense of personal, physical, and financial independence from the suffocating mise-en-scène commonly established by one's curfew-keepers. Even so, the fact that Yvette's guardians hadn't attempted to manipulate her emotionally by laying heavy guilt trips on her for having made such a recklessly rash, impulsive, and potentially foolhardy decision that might easily prove short-sighted in the long run—as most loving, affectionate, kindhearted, well-meaning adoptive parents were not disinclined to do—somehow or other rubbed our pampered young princess the wrong way for reasons she had immense difficulty decoding. For the sake of form, Yvette Cartier still put on an act of being a diligent, hard-working student by hiring Dr. Dweebaldo Van Boofus on retainer to do virtually all of her school assignments in her behalf, in despite of the handsome fees he charged for his services. She would remunerate him hebdomadally with funds she withdrew at regular intervals from offshore bank accounts that overflowed with the generous assets she received from her Great Uncle Weaser, like clockwork, on the first of every month. It had never occurred to her to question the sustainability of such an arrangement, an unfortunate oversight that would be not unmarkedly to her grave detriment in due course.

She had learnt from experience, and from empirical observation, that it was strategically imperative to exercise what are commonly referred to as "flexible ethics" (i.e., a way of practicing the doing of what is convenient rather than what is right) when it came to performing her class assignments, rationalizing that the predominant majority of other students also subscribed to the selfsame ideology as a shrewd survival tactic in the dog-eat-dog world of academe, and that those with the financial resources were usually far better equipped to escape detection, and therethrough avoid any adverse consequences for their "flexibly ethical" practices, than the poverty-stricken down-and-outers who relied on high-interest loans to pay off their incrementally mounting student debts.

Be that as it may, unlike her easy-going, laid-back, over-permissive guardians, her neo-Victorian governess Prunelda had a tendency to invade Yvette's privacy way far too often by asking her a whole slew of prying and personal questions— more like interrogations (or "inquisigations," as Yvette coined them)—and there were times as well when her governess would walk in on her without knocking, when our heroine happened to be alone in her bedchamber, which she found not only maddeningly unnerving but also nettlesomely obnoxious in all respects. As there was no security chain or deadbolt latch on her bedroom door, it was prac- tically impossible for her to find time to paddle her pink canoe without the gnawing anxiety that Prunelda would barge in on her unannounced, which was one of the primary reasons our heroine felt enormously grateful to have finally found the peace & quiet she'd so desperately craved for her "me-time" (as she termed it).

From what she had thus far been able to garner, Celine had only showed up once or twice a week to collect her phone messages, and that was usually towards the end of Yvette's work shift. Upon moving out of her guardian's house and finally having a place she could truly call her own, she felt as though she had turned a significant new leaf in her life and absolutely relished every minute of it! As things stood at the moment, she was unaccountable to anyone except her boss-cum-supervisor Celine, which was really no big deal at all, seeing as how little she demanded of her. As for Eiden, Yvette could do whatever she pleased in his presence, even (or especially) if it incurred his affected displeasure, for his ostensible "punishments," as they stood, were more like heavenly rewards, from her tilted perverspective, howsoever biased she may have in sooth been as an affectatiously unwilling recipient thereof. And, since the two of them were essentially on the same wavelength, they understood this dynamic amazingly well, even to the point where they never really had to talk about it, for they could communicate quite effectively by literally reading each other's minds, often by means of subtle unconscious signalings in their body language in the form of micro-expressions, non-verbal leakages, facial mannerisms and suchlike.

All these thoughts cascaded through her head as she kept Eiden waiting in the bedroom for more than two hours whilst enjoying the built-in Delta TempAssure Thermostatic Shower System with its integrated volume control and multiple body sprays. When she finally stepped out of the shower she didn't bother to towel herself off, since she knew it thrilled Eiden no end whenever she was dripping wet and feeling deliciously chilly (he would often turn up the air conditioning system to play up the "thrill of the chill," so to speak)—and it spinned her dials as well, as it made her all the more heedful of how unequivocally vulnerable she was in his commanding presence. She couldn't wait to feel Eiden's cool firm hand on her nude backside as he mock-scolded and spanked her for taking up too much of his valuable time.

When she stepped into her bedroom, clean-as-a-whistle, half expecting her lover to pounce upon her, she felt a subitous wave of discombobulation upon sur-realizing that he was nowhere to be seen. Something, in fact, felt terribly, terribly wrong. She discovered an upside-down smiley-face sticky note on the refrigerator door informing her that he had taken her clothes to the dry cleaners to have them laundered and would return them in a jiff. She felt a faint stab of panic, however, when she cast her eyes about the bedroom. The first thing she noticed was that all the bedclothes had been stripped off the croc leather futon. Her street clothes were no longer hanging over the armchair where she had left them prior to her late-morning ablutions. She looked through her dresser drawers only to discover, to her incredulous dismay, that there wasn't a stitch of clothing to be found anywhere inside them, not so much as even a choker or a garter belt. Opening the door to her wardrobe closet, she found nothing but empty hangers. In fact, the only item left in her apartment that she could actually put on was a pair of black patent leather Christian Louboutin high-heeled shoes from Saks Fifth Avenue.

In a last ditch effort to find some covering to make herself halfways decent she looked in the bathroom where she discovered, to her speechless consternation, that all the towels had been removed from their racks. Even the toilet tissue dispenser had been emptied! The thermostat controlling the central air conditioning had been turned down to 50 degrees Fahrenheit and, if that wasn't bad enough, she noticed, to her chagrin, that the key to the thermostat had been withdrawn and was nowhere to be found, making it impossible for her to manipulate its temperature setting. The cold draught wouldn't have bothered her so much if Eiden had been there to light her fire, so to speak. Where in hell was he, anyway...? she wondered.

She did a double-take of the mind at the shocking yet sobering surrealization that there wasn't a single solitary stitch, thread, or tallywagger of anything at all whatsoever in any nook or cranny of her apartment wherewith she could shield herself from the prospective thrice-overs of ogling wink-a-peeps, goosings of groping fists, or friggings of ginormous rubber penises, making her feel small, like an unwelcome trespasser in her own living quarters. Yvette was unable to get a handle on the whys and wherefores of her significant other's having gone to the unnecessary trouble of taking hundreds of articles of her clothing to the dry cleaners, especially as the overwhelming preponderance of said garments still had price tags appended to them, with no need at all of being washed as they hadn't even yet been worn.

Never in all her life had she felt so utterly defenseless and vulnerable—a feeling intensified by the continuous currents of cold air blasting down at her from the vents in the ceiling. What in the depths of darkness would she do if there was a sudden emergency that would call for her to evacuate the premises without delay? she wondered. Still dripping wet from her shower, she had no way to dry herself off, which only served to exacerbate her crippling sense of self-consciousness. Her apartment didn't feel like a home at the moment but rather more like a commercial office space: cold and impersonal, as if it had only recently been vacated by its previous occupants and staged by a property management company for the purpose of attracting new tenants.

And then it struck her asudden: her cellphone! Of course! Like, *duh!!!* She could call Eiden straightaway to cue him in on the precarious predicament in which she currently found herself. He would be her champion, her savior! Why hadn't she been more quick on the uptake to have considered that option in the first place? she wondered. Prior to berating herself, however, for being so impenetrably dense, she surrealized on the spot that she may have been subconsciously hesitant to call him for a compelling reason, namely: the question as to whether this was merely an instance of careless presumptuousness on his part, i.e., that, in his eagerness to please her, he had run off with all her clothing and, in a fit of absentmindedness, neglected to give her any advance warning thereof, much less leave her with at least a single suitable ensemble she could slip on ad interim. Perhaps he had meant, in all innocence (as an act of unalloyed love, no less), to pleasantly surprise her with a batch of fresh-laundered raiment. Or worse: maybe it was a premeditated mischievous prank on his part, in which case the obvious question raised would be whether he was trying to up the ante in his role-playing as the dom in their relationship or was, peradventure, taking a poke at humiliating her sexually at an even higher level of psycho-emotional severity, specifically: that he was ratcheting up her level of shame, embarrassment, and sheer vulnerability as a ruse to capture her heart so that she would be forever beholden to him (?). She was uncertain at this point as to whether she loved this man with all her heart or resented him with all her spleen. At the moment she was more inclined to gravitate towards the latter sentiment, namely: that she abhorred the very ground he tread upon for having put her (inadvertingly or no) into such a pretty pickle.

Yvette stepped over to the nightstand by her futon to snatch the cellphone she had left on her charger overnight only to discover, to her grim despair, that it, too, had been swiped, which made her heart sink even deeper into her chest, for the subintelligence undergirding such a furacious maneuver didn't bode well for her demur in the odd-come-shortly. What if Eiden were to get himself into an auto— or worse, a wingsuit-flying—accident? she mused. What would she do *then...?* The only other option she could think of at the moment was to try and figure out how to make outgoing calls on the landline on her work desk, until she was hit afresh with the discomfiting surrealization that her boss had nearabout bent over backwards to make a distinctly emphatic point (a bit of a song & dance, actually, as if she'd had a humungous axe to grind for reasons our distraught nymphette was unable to fathom) of informing Yvette that the phone was only set up for incoming, not outgoing, calls.

Our subdebutante was so beside herself with disconcertion at this point that she had forgotten momentarily that her work shift was scheduled to start in less than twenty minutes. Unless she could figure out a way to pull herself out of the pot she was in, she would have no choice but to station herself at the desk to answer each and every incoming call, as 'twas absolutely imperative she do so lest she risk getting kicked off her gravy train—the McJob of her dreams, no less. Aside from being all decked out in her birthday suit, our panicked young subdebutante now found herself devoid of her only viable channels of communication with the outside world. This meant that she would just have to sit there doing naught but twiddle her thumbs whilst fretting over the perilous clusterfuck in which she'd just landed herself front and center.

Thus far, there hadn't been more than one or two calls per day coming in, which were mostly from distributors arranging times for deliveries and/or pickups from the adjoining warehouse, which, thankfully, she was not under any obligation to deal with directly, as physically meeting the delivery servicemen wasn't a part of her job description (or so she had hithertills presumed). The main concern she had at the moment was that her boss might pop in on her casually to see how things were going, or to simply pick up her messages, which she hadn't done in the past several days. The rare occasions that Celine had dropped in on Yvette had thus far occurred towards the end of her work shifts, usually just a minute or two before she clocked out for the day. She hoped against all hope that Eiden would return her clean laundry by then. Which made her wonder anew: Where on earth was he anyway...? Why the devil was it taking him so long to return with her laundry...? She near-about threw her stomach when assailed by the half-formed figment that her lover might be two- or even three-timing her behind her back. Sensing Eiden's duplicitous, nay, triplicitous nature, she wouldn't necessarily put it past him to play her for a fool. What if he had been gifting his girlfriends on the side with her fine and fancy raiment, which included hundreds of as yet unwrapped elite-brand ensembles that had been hanging in her wardrobe for weeks, if not months? Heaven forfend! Banish the very thought of such a treacherous betrayal!

Whilst distracted by her unsettled mindset, it struck Yvette, all of a heap, that it may not be such a bad idea to conceal the hundreds of items she had nicked from the adjoining warehouse, notwithstanding Eiden's bland reassurances that she had had Celine's tacit permission, even her unmitigated blessing, to help herself without encumbrance to anything soever she desired. Even so, our subdebutante feared, not without justification, that she might have overstayed her welcome in that department.

All these tumultuous thoughts swirled through her psyche when she was startled asudden by the strident buzz-like ring of the landline chatterbox on her work desk. Bloody hell! she thought. It's already 12:00 o'clock! She took a deep breath before picking up the receiver and answering the phone as calmly and professionally as she could, taking under consideration the harrowing circumstances in which she now found herself.

"Hello, this is Yvette. May I ask who's calling please?"

"Ah, Yvette! I'm so glad I was able to reach you. I have your term paper ready and thought I could hand-deliver it to you straightaway, as I happen to be in your neck o' the woods. In fact, I'm standing just kitty-corner across the street from the love toy warehouse where I was told you were working, but I'll be damned if I can find the front entrance to the place. Would you kindly let me know how I can reach your doorstep?"

Yvette froze like a deer in a headlight, and then, in a quick jerk, hit the dial. She had forgotten that Dr. Dweebaldo Van Boofus had been scheduled to turn in her paper today at noon on the nose.

The phone rang again, and even though she knew that, in all probability, it was Dr. Van Boofus calling her back, she dared not run the risk of *failing* to pick up the receiver, lest she forfeit her employment thereby. "Think, Yvette, think ... think ... think quick!" she mumbled to herself, notwithstanding that, in despite of racking her brains, she drew naught but a big blank, as if in a state of utter obliviation.

"Hello?" she answered more cautiously, without identifying herself.

"Yvette! Long time no see! It's Werther. I have something of the utmost importance to impart to thee. I—" She slammed the phone down as hard as she could, feeling both flustered and furious that her nominal "ex" would dare call her— especially at her new place of employ. As far as she was concerned, the two of them were finished for good and all. She never wanted to see his face or hear his voice again as long as she lived, intolerable crashing bore that he was! If he continued calling her in this manner (as he had on numerous other occasions at her guardians' home, as well as on her private cell), she would have no choice but to report him to the authorities for stalking & harassing her, and arrange, if necessary, to submit an application for a restraining order against him ... t*he bloody sonuvabitch!*

The phone rang yet again. Three calls in a row? she grumbled, beside herself with vexation. Why was this happening *now?* This time she made a snap decision not to pick up, assuming ten to one it was Werther trying his luck at reaching her a second time. Howbeit, when she heard her lover's voice on the answering machine, she scrambled in desperation to take the call, until it dawned on her, to her hopeless dismay, that she hadn't been trained as to which codes to punch in and/or buttons to press on the keypad that would enable her to establish one-on-one communication with callers who were in the process of relaying messages on the machine, most probably on the assumption that it was not the sort of thing she would ever have been expected to do whilst on the job, seeing as there was a tacit understanding with her employer that she pick up each and every call, without fail, before the second ring. Yvette was practically foaming at the mouth with frustration at her monstrous stupidity, such that she started shedding tears of despair upon hearing the sweet message of her lover in real time on the answering machine.

"Hi Babe," said Eiden, "I thought you were working today but since you're not picking up, I'll have to assume you went out somewhere. Hope you're enjoying yourself on this beautiful crisp cool autumn day! Even though it's chilly outside, I have to say I just love these brisk November afternoons when the sun's shining bright through puffy white clouds and there's a stiff breeze off the ocean with a hint of snow in the offing. I was going to leave a bag of clean laundry at your apartment just now but since you're not there, I'll leave it at your guardians' home instead. Call me when you get a chance. Love you, Sweetie!"

She heard the fatal click before she was able to so much as even begin to set forth on attempting to figure out if there was any feasible way in the world she could catch him on the line in advance of his terminating the call. Accreasingly, she had the gnawing sensation that she was, as the saying goes, "up shit creek without a paddle," although in her particular case, if the proverbial "paddle" were to materialize anywhere within spanking reach of her exposed anatomy, it would by all odds be administered (and, she feared, in nowise unrobustly) upon the blind cheeks of her unfledged ultimatum.

The phone rang immediately thereafter, which made her shudder with apprehension. Crossing her fingers that it was Eiden calling her back, she picked up the receiver only to hear the voice of his sister, Celine. "Hey there, Yvette, I just wanted to check in on you to make sure everything's okay. I just ran into Dweebaldo Van Boofus across the street from where you are. He told me he's a long-time acquaintance of yours. He's standing outside the warehouse right now as we speak and told me he just tried calling you, and that you picked up, but that the line had suddenly gone dead for some strange and inexplicable reason—a baffling mystery, to be sure, which, quite frankly, is totally beyond me, as no such thing has ever been known to occur in these parts, at least, according to the half-dozen telephone service providers I just spoke with, all of whose managers reassured me there were no traceable glitches in the operating system from their end but that they would immediately forward my message to the FBI and Department of Homeland Insecurity, both agencies of which are far better equipped to research this unaccountable malfunction. Dr. Van Boofus and I both expressed our deep concerns to one another that there might be something amiss going on inside the building. This phone glitch, if in fact that's what it is, could quite possibly be attributable to some faulty wiring in your apartment or, percase, a leak in the roof (which, in and of itself, would be strikingly irregular, to say the least, especially since it hasn't rained here in over a month). Of course, it could be something even more serious than that. Are you sure everything's alright in your neck o' the woods...?"

Before Yvette could gather her thoughts to fabricate a suitable fib to save face in response to Celine's solicitous query, her boss pressed on as if she had only meant her question to be taken rhetorically, which our nonplussed ingénude found, in and of itself, to be not a little unnerving. "If there is a problem with the telephone," said Celine, "I'll send in a team of service repairmen to fix it on the double. On the other hand, in the unlikely event that we should receive evacuation orders from the building's management team, the fire department, Emergency Response, FEMA, Homeland Insecurity or whatever, you can rest assured that I will personally see to it that you are the very first party notified, so make sure you sit tight for the nonce, just in case. In any event, Dr. Van Boofus told me he wanted to deliver your term paper to you for Professor Xeroxburger's Astrophysiology class, which he said, according to what you told him, is due tomorrow morning at 8:00 o'clock sharp. He said it's urgent that he bring it to you posthaste and collect his two-thousand dollar fee, preferably in low denominations (by the way, two thousand bucks for a ten-page term paper...? That's pretty steep, if you ask me. I've no doubt there are some quality essay writing services out there that wouldn't charge you even a tenth that amount, but I guess that's not really my business. Just saying ...). Anyhow, Dr. Van Boofus wanted me to convey to you that, as it is evidently highly unlikely that he would be able to squeeze in another slot of time in his hectic schedule to hand-deliver the paper to you until late next week, long after it's due, he wanted me to ask you if it's okay that I show him the way to the front doorstep of your apartment. Also, if you don't mind, I'd like to tag along with him, as there are some matterable issues of earthshaking ponderance I would like to discuss with you face to face."

Before our heroine could get a word in edgewise, her boss hung up on her. Yvette was none too pleased to have learned that Dr. Van Boofus had been so carelessly cavalier in respect to the rules of their signed contract of confidentiality in connection with the term papers she had paid him on retainer to ghostwrite in her behalf. It was outrageous beyond belief that he had taken it upon himself to disclose any information whithersoever apropos of their ongoing clandestine business relationship, especially to her employer, who just so happened to be on a first-name basis with the wife of the dean & president of Pimpleton State: Helga Armstrong. What if tongues started wagging about the fact that Yvette routinely hired ghostwriters to compose all her research papers and complete all her class assignments? And, moreover, what if so much as the faintest susurration of such hearsay (malicious or no), the merest soupçon of such twittle-twattle (spiteful or no), or the remotest suspicion of such scandalous-sounding clish-ma-claver drifted back to the august offices of the dean & president of Pimpleton State: Herr Professor Ulrich Armstrong? What would happen *then?* she brooded. *What then...?*

Downcast and onion-eyed with heat-drops of shame streaming down her physiognomy onto her blait begonias, Yvette dreaded the inevitable moment she would be discovered in her unfledged state, which she imagined could happen at any moment now. Celine had the keys to Yvette's apartment and could walk right in on her unannounced if she felt the inclination to do so.

Suddenly and unexpectedly, there was a violent thumping of what sounded like a clenched, brass-knuckled fist on the front door of her apartment. It goes without saying that, figuratively speaking, it scared the pants off of her in despite of the fact that she had none on her. The stentorious pounding was heavy and persistent. "Let me in, Yvette! I have something of the utmost importance to impart to thee! Make haste! I beg of thee! It's urgent!"

Half relieved and half disgusted, she immediately recognized the nasal adenoidal vox of her "ex"—Werther Nemesinovich. There was no way in hell she would ever open the door for *him,* even if she were dressed to the nines to paint the town red. She was afraid, however, that he might make an ugly scene in front of her boss and Dr. Van Boofus, both of whom were apparently on their way to her front doorstep this very moment.

Yvette was resigned, at this stage of the game, to losing her coveted position but also somewhat relieved that her boss (who was, by all accounts, a very decent human being) would be able to contact Eiden so that she could get her clean laundry returned to her in short order. Yes, it would be incredibly embarrassing, even humiliating, but, at this juncture, she just wanted the worst of it to be over and done with, come what may.

Werther pounded on the door a second time, knowing full well that Yvette was inside her apartment.

"Go away!" she cried. "Just leave me alone!"

"I love you, Yvette, with all my heart!" cried Werther. "I'll do anything for you! Anything at all! Just ask me and it's yours! Your wish is my command!"

A new voice sounded from outside her door—a stern authoritative voice she recognized immediately as the dean and president of her school, Professor Ulrich Armstrong. "What's going on here?" he asked Werther.

"Nothing, sir. None of your business."

"Whoa!" thought Yvette. "That guy's got some big nuts on him to talk back to the dean that way."

"I'm afraid it *is* my business, son. I need to have a serious word with this young lady about some urgent issues regarding her academic performance at the luniversity, so I suggest you move along, as this is a deeply confidential matter."

It sounded, to Yvette's ears, as though a violent altercation was in the works until she made out the voice of her boss at the top of the stairwell directing Dr. Van Boofus (her ostensibly "anonymous" ghostwriter) to the front door of her digs.

"Right this way, sir. I'll accompany you there as I need to speak with her as well."

Yvette heard a steely hardness in Celine's voice that made her feel especially anxious and uncomfortable. There were dozens of half-empty bottles of sex lubricants in her bedroom, not to mention vibrators and dildos that she hadn't found time to stash away in the drawers of her cabinet—all the sorts of items she would rather no one see, especially her boss, who had an imperiously authoritative way about her that Yvette found not a little unsettling. Our flustered coquette was still seated at her desk, naked as a jay-bird's ass and afraid to move lest she make her situation even more unfewsome thereby.

"Greetings Ulrich, what brings you here?" asked Celine, who at this point was standing just outside the front door to Yvette's apartment.

"Ulrich...?" thought Yvette with mounting alarm. She had no idea that her boss was on a first-name basis with the dean and president of her school. "On the other hand," she reasoned to herself, "why wouldn't she be, as she already appeared to be on intimate terms with his wife Helga?" In fact, Celine had addressed the dean with such casual familiarity (Yvette could even overhear the slurpy smooching sounds of kisses being exchanged on their cheeks, if not their lips), that our heroine could not help but wonder if the two of them had once been an item or if, mayhaps, they had a clandestine affair currently underway. The very thought of such a thing made her feel not a little green-eyed, as Professor Armstrong was a man—tall, stern, and handsome (not to mention rich, strong, and powerful)—for whom Yvette herself had long had the hots. If there had been a thing going on between Professor Armstrong and Celine Dreadmiller, how would Helga—the president and dean's wife of over twenty years—have reacted to getting wind of such an entanglement? Perhaps, our heroine conjectured, there had been a major scandal in the pipeline that had been kept under wraps with hush money payments from Professor Armstrong to Celine Dreadmiller. How else could her boss, a mere graduate student at the Pimpleton Heights Academy of Art & Design, have been able to afford such a fancy supercar, let alone the high-end business she owned and managed? For that matter, how could she afford to pay our heroine a staggering $666.00 per hour for doing diddly-squat?

Although the town of Pimpleton Heights was an affluent suburb of the greater Pimpleton retropolitan area, it still maintained something of a small-town ambience with all the petty small-town power struggles embedded in its political fabric. Everyone seemed to know each other as well. Somehow, she felt that, whether or not Celine Dreadmiller and Ulrich Armstrong had been romantically involved, the very fact that they were on a friendly foot with each other didn't exactly augur well for the outcome of our ungarbed Delilah's sticky dilemma. In quiet desperation, she deluded herself into believing, one way or another, that getting wind of this possible scandal might afford her some leverage that would enable her to squeeze her way out of the tight spot she was in.

Fat friggin' chance! pronunciated a tremulous vox from deep inside the murkiest recesses of her soul.

"Well, truth be told," answered Dean & President Armstrong, "I'm here to relay some excellent news to Ms. Cartier about a prestigious scholarship she's been awarded, and I felt it incumbent upon me to pay her a personal visit to offer her my heartiest congratulations, especially as it reflects so well on the reputation of our luniversity, raising its stock significantly in terms of bringing international recognition to our students and faculty for their stellar academic achievements— and Mademoiselle Cartier is at the very top of the A-list in our student body. Her scholarly work has been peer-reviewed world-wide and found to be absolutely glowing at the highest attainable standard. Her original research has already been shown to have had a profoundly significant influence on the best known scholars in her field. It would be no overstatement to say that the award being conferred upon Ms. Cartier is on an equal par with a MacArthur Fellowship (also known as the 'genius grant') in terms of the sheer magnitude of its monetary reward and all the prestige that goes along with it, which, I dare say, is no small deal in these parts."

Yvette was allutterly flabbergasted by what she was hearing. *How could this possibly be?* she wondered. Now, as she could hear explicitly through the door (a door of such cheap quality, by the way, that it would be easy enough for anyone to kick it straight open), it was Dr. Van Boofus who chimed in before Celine had a chance to offer the dean & president her respectful congratulations. "Professor Armstrong, do you know who I am?"

"You look vaguely familiar to me, sir. I apologize that I can't remember your name," replied Professor Armstrong.

"Dweebaldo Van Boofus, Professor. I took several courses of yours as a doctoral student at Pimpleton State over twenty years ago. Upon my graduation from there (*summa cum laude,* I might add) back in 2003, I applied for several tenure-track appointments at your school. Unfortunately, I was never accepted for any of those positions. I've had to grind out a modest living over the years as a ghostwriter for students at Pimpleton State. I'm telling you this because I want to express to you that I'm mightily astonished to hear you mention that Mademoiselle Yvette Cartier is slated to win a prestigious prize (if, as you claim, it's on an equal par with the MacArthur Fellowship, then it would stand to reason that it must be myriad leagues beyond a Guggenheim or a Pulitzer in terms of the revenue being awarded, never mind the professional prestige it would presumably bring to its awardee), especially as I can inform thee with unwavering confidence, nay, with absolute certainty, sir, that Ms. Cartier is neither a scholar, by any stretch of the imagination, nor an expert in anything other than her own insatiable materialistic cravings. She is naught but a conceited, mardy, snobby, entitled, impudent, spoilt little rich brat who deserves nothing better than to be summarily stripped down to her queen of holes and whipped on her faceable antipodes on a movable rotating turntable, set tall upon an elevated platform in the town square, before all the high-minded, upstanding, irreproachable inhabitants of our progressive municipality for the purpose of exposing her unspeakable malefactions and offenses to every Tom, Dick & Mary within these parts and abroad, and inculcated simultaneously with a stern albeit instructive lesson in everlasting shame, submission, and repentance so that she'll learn to mind her P's & Q's once and for all. End of discussion! Furtherover, as far as her soi-disant academic scholarship goes, she's an actionable fraud!

"I'm telling you this because I think it's important for you to know that Mademoiselle Cartier has been my number one client for the past two and a half years. I have been writing all of her research papers and essays and doing most of her class assignments at her behest since she was a junior in prep school. And, in the event that you're skeptical of what I'm imparting unto thee, I have here in my possession a completed term paper assignment she commissioned from me last week, which I just composed for her late last night, and which is due at 8:00 o'clock sharp tomorrow morning in Professor Druben Xeroxburger's astrophysiology class. I was just about to hand-deliver it to Ms. Cartier this very instant; however, upon hearing you go into raptures about her bogus academic achievements, I must say that I now have some serious second thoughts about doing so. Here, take a look at it yourself, in case you don't believe me."

Dweebaldo Van Boofus handed over the ten-page term paper, along with a detailed contract bearing Yvette's signature, to Professor Armstrong, who accepted it with grudging skepticism.

"Now, please know," continued Dr. Van Boofus, before Professor Armstrong had a chance to get a word in edgewise, "that under ordinary berserkumstances, I wouldn't choose to divulge such information to anyone, especially to the dean and president of my client's school, as I'm under contract to keep the business relationship I have with her strictly confidential (a contract that would never hold up in court, by the way, considering how things have stood between us), but I have to admit to you, sir, that I'm positively sick & tired of never receiving so much as even a smidgen of credit for my scholarly work. I have kept digital files and hard copies of every single assignment I have been commissioned to write in Ms. Cartier's behalf, along with all the receipts for the fees I have charged her over the years, so I can prove my case in court if I ever need to. I just want to make it perfectly clear to you, Professor Armstrong, that if anybody at all is qualified to be awarded the scholarship you have just described, I am, in sooth, that individual. I think, in fact, it's high time that you and your illustrious colleagues seriously consider hiring me for an endowed tenured professorship at your luniveristy. The field of study makes absolutely no difference to me, as I am a prolific polymath; that is to say, I am expertly versed in a multitude of subjects. I am neither an idiot savant nor a megasavant nor an "A-to-Z man" like the Autodidact in Sartre's *Nausea* (the character who reads every single book in the library in alphabetical order). I am flexibly-minded insofar as taking both a prescriptivist and descriptivist approach to linguistics, which extends into my thinking on history & literature as well as in the arts & sciences."

For about fifteen minutes there was a silence behind the door so thick you could slice it with a machete. Yvette could overhear the crinkling of the sheets of her commissioned term paper and its accompanying signed contract being scrupulously pored over from one page to the next, interspersed with occasional huffs and shrieks of outrage, by the parties assembled on the threshold of her doorstep. The idea occurred to her then and there to lock herself in the bathroom to delay being found in her present condition until she recomembered, to her woebegone discumfuddlement, that the lock on the bathroom door had been accidentally busted by Eiden the other day when the the two of them had gone a bit overboard during one of their role-playing sessions. Thus, she was left with no alternative now but to quietly sit at her work desk, in meek resignation, to await her moment of moral reckoning. The breathless silence was finally broken by the husky male voice of a complete stranger announcing to Celine Dreadmiller that he was there to pick up a delivery from the warehouse.

"Gentlemen, hold tight for a moment," said Celine. "I have to tend to some pressing business. I'll be right back." Yvette could hear the stormtrooper-like clops of Celine's high heels as they echoed down through the length of the cavernous warehouse towards a section at the far end thereof where some of the most expensive articles of merchandise were stored, followed a minute thereafter by a sudden and violent stream of strange and colorful expletives being barked by Celine's incisively penetrating melodramatic operatic voice. The clops of her high heels got louder and louder as they approached Yvette's doorstep once again, this time at a hell-for-leather stride.

There was an abrupt, brutal, percussive succession of thunderous knocks with ironlike fists on Yvette's seeming balsa-wood door followed by Celine's tyrannically outraged aristobombastic voice. "Yvette, open up! Open the door—*pronto!* I need to have a strict word with you—*now!*" Our disconcerted subdebutante sat silent as a saint and still as a statue in the hopes that her boss and all the others would simply give up and go home. Howbeit, alas, her efforts in that direction proved to no avail. "Yvette!" shouted her boss. "I know you're in there! I can hear you hyperventilating, you bad, *bad,* naughty little girl! Open up the door this instant or I'm coming in along with three demanding musclemen who would also like to have a hard-and-fast word with you. D'ya hear me?!" Celine pounded on the door again to the point where it sounded as though it would split in two at any moment. The next succession of knocks were not only with fists but also with the kicks of sturdy boots that most probably belonged to the delivery serviceman. Just before Yvette feared that the door would be knocked off its hinges, she heard the dread sound of keys rattling on a chain.

CHAPTER ELEVEN

Yvette, in tears and with a lovely rosy blush suffusing her cheeks, covered her nakedness with her bare hands in abject shame when the door flew wide open.

Celine froze in shock upon seeing her employee not only out of uniform but wearing naught but a tearful pout on her fresh young face.

"What the fork...?" exclaimed Celine before breaking out into contemptuous laughter that proved infectious insofar as the three musclemen accompanying her were quick off the mark to band together with her as accessories in her flink of scornful mirth at the sight of our disgraced young heroine cowering at her work desk in naught but her birthday suit. Celine, who was sharp as a tack and swift as a lightning bolt—being the maniacal speed demon she most assuredly was (especially in view of how she drove her fancy schmancy supercar)—took in the room in a flash and immediately zeroed in on the mess of half empty bottles, open cardboard containers, sex toys of all shapes, forms, and sizes (including a pair of handcuffs) that were scattered all over the bedchamber.

Yvette, for the very first time in her life, came to the dramatically abrupt, if not bluntly rude, surrealization that there was a fundamental qualitative distinction to be made between the fun little role-playing rituals she enacted with her lover and bona fide, real-world, no-holds-barred Embarrassment with a capital B. Yvette hoped against all hope that Celine would have the heart somewhere inside her to empathize with her predicament, at least to the point where she would see fit to call her brother on her mobile device to beg him to return her clean laundry so that she could, at very least, be vouchsafed the dignity of being permitted to put some clothes on before having to submit herself to the stern dressing down she knew instinctively was about to befall her. Our helpless subdebutante's throat tightened to the point where she could barely so much as even squeak like a baby squirrel in her defense.

"What the devil do you think you're doing?" Celine called out in a powerful operatic soprano vox on a par with Jessye Norman singing Schönberg's *Erwartung* that was sufficiently stentorious such that anyone in the adjoining warehouse and parking lot directly above it could hear the incisively enunciated phonemes of her merciless excoriations resonating therethrough with a clarity so sharp, they could just as well have been listening to her tirades of abuse on a pair of Focal Utopia headphones in an insulated sound chamber proofed with egg cartons. "I have a de-livery serviceman here to pick up an order and he just informed me that at least half the merchandise has gone missing. Now I can see, clear as a bell, what's been going on here, you disgusting little skank!"

Blushing as scarlet as a Victor Hugo rose in springtime, Yvette bent forward in her chair in a futilitous indeavearance to bescreen her charms with naught but her bare hands in a pathetic show of female modesty. She was unable to formulate, let alone articulate, any excuses whatsoever to account for all the confirmatory evidence of her licentious conduct.

Celine Dreadmiller, not one known for mincing words, pointed towards the mess of stolen inventory scattered all over the bedchamber. "How do you explain this?" she asked. "What in the world do you have to say for yourself, young lady, *huh...?* What in the name of all the Holy Saints and Martyrs makes you think for even so much as a split fraction of a second that you can get away with this despicable immoral behavior without repercussions? You obscene, self-serving, lascivious little slut!"

Celine's harsh words felt to our heroine like honed knife-blades piercing through her flesh.

"What do you take me for anyways?" demanded Celine. "A blind obliviot...? A doofless duncehead...? An incompetent, clay-brained clinchpoop...? An ignorant little ning-nong...? An airheaded half-wit...? Do you honestly think I don't keep track of every single item I purchase...? That I'm a sloppy book-keeper, percase...? That somehow or other I've been remiss in maintaining a general ledger of each & every transaction I execute—debits & credits, howsoever infinitesimally minuscule they might chance to be—pertaining to my business expenditures...? Are you trying to insinuate by your actions that I cheat on my corporate tax returns...?" Celine Dreadmiller's voice crescendoed from a fortissimo to a fortissisisimo. "How *dare* thee!!! Dost thou make so bold as to imagine in your wildest wet dreams that your guardian devil is going to protect thee by pampering your pea-sized guilty conscience with its suave reassurances that there's no way in the darkest corners of hell I would ever take cognizance of such a precipitous drop in mine inventory...?"

Dr. Dweebaldo Van Boofus, President Ulrich Armstrong, and the delivery serviceman insinuated themselves into Yvette's apartment, all but filling the space with their brawny masculine physiques, and cast our discomfited subdebutante a collective gaze of stern disapprobation mingled with what she could not help but sense was a tinct of insatiable concupiscence.

"I ... I'm sorry." squeaked Yvette pathetically whilst trying to cover the nipples on her breasts with her bare hands only to surrealize that her Brazilian waxed pudenda were completely exposed. She had to use her right arm to cover her breasts and her left hand to shield her vulva, leaving the cleft betwixt her butt cheeks open for public scrutiny.

"Whaddya mean you're 'sorry?'" snarled Celine in her tinkler's tongue. "Feelin' 'sorry' ain't gonna bring back my inventory now, is it?"

"N-n-no ma'am,'" squeaked Yvette in a mousy little voice, tears of remorse streaming down her visage onto her unclothed cleavage, atwixt her twin lovelies.

"Don't you dare think for so much as even an instant that I don't know exactly what you've been doing here all day and all night, thou shameless, soiled, wicked little wench! It's indecent, it's deplorable, and absogoddamnlutely disgusting! Fie on thee, thou stinkin' nasty, muddy little harlot! And woe betide thee if thou even durst so much as deny what's as patently conspectable as that weepin' little baby in yer boat down there, thou intemperately loose little nympho!" Celine Dreadmiller yanked Yvette's left palm away from the pleasure pearl it was shielding and pointed her sharp-nailed dexter index at our heroine's exposed clitoris. "Didst thou not even bother to read the fine print in the contract you signed with my company?"

"N-n-n-no, ma'am, I-I-I'm afraid not," Yvette answered pathetically in barely audible little pips.

"N-n-n-n-n-no, mu'am, I-I-I-I'm afwaid not," Celine repeated, mocking Yvette's high squeaky stuttering coloratura voice. The delivery serviceman snickered, followed by muffled sniggles and snorts from Dr. Dweebaldo Van Boofus and Professor Ulrich Armstrong. "Failing to read the fine print on contracts doesn't quite cut it in these parts now, does it, young lady?"

"P-p-please ma'am, I-I-I'm really sorry. Eiden went off with all my laundry and hasn't had a chance to return it yet," she said in a lame effort to explain her shameless nudity.

"That's absolutely untrue, thou impudent lying little sneak! I heard my brother's message to thee loud and clear on the answering machine just a few short minutes ago! He tried to call you on this very landline and you deliberately—with phallus aforethought no doubt—made the unilateral decision not to answer it, which is what I've been breaking my back paying you to do, thou mendacious little bimbo! Such flagrant refusal to follow my orders constitutes willful insubordination. If you had read the contract more scrupulously, let alone at all, you would know that failure to answer this telephone even *once*, let alone after the second ring, is unforgivable and grounds not only for your immediate dismissal but also for being henceforth blacklisted from any other McJobs related to this profession (to say nothing of the overwhelming preponderance of those that aren't) for ever and after, *capeesh?* Morefurther, as stated in the contract, greasing your gash on the premises is strictly verboten and punishable with the severest of penalties, including (especially in extreme cases such as your own) being modeled around the city for sport. And, if deemed advisable, this rod in a pickle is enforced with the strictest practicable rigor and vigor—*I kid thee not!*"

Like a mad counter-clockwise rotating tornado from hell, Celine was at the opposite end of the room unlatching the door to Yvette's wardrobe closet, whereupon, at lightning speed she returned in a virtual cyclonic rotation, within the blink of an eye, vambrashing Yvette's pair of black patent leather Christian Louboutin high-heeled shoes from Saks Fifth Avenue in her right hand. "Put them on!" she commanded. "*Now!*"

At this juncture, our disgraced young coquette felt a nowise unpronounced disinclination to embrace what she perceived to be the general tenor of Celine's verbal utterances and what they came across as signifying for her personal future. To wear high-heeled shoes and nothing else would only serve to aggravate rather than alleviate her wholesale sense of being unabashedly bare-skinned, insofar as they would serve to enclose her Sunday suit in a frame of sorts, officializing it as if it were a painting in a gallery. It would make her look less like an article of virtue and more like a common cum dumpster. 'Twas therefore with only the meekest of reluctance that Yvette obtemperated to her boss's distasteful request. As a brave if not foolhardy act of rebellious defiance (having momentaneously disremembered that Celine was not in fact her schoolmarmy governess Prunelda), our heroine intentionally took more time than was necessary to strap on the dispendious stilettos, which earned her a sharp smack on the duff, catching her completely off guard.

"Quit monkeying around, you silly-born, doofless retardo!" shouted Celine. "We haven't got all day!" Her tone of voice made it abundantly clear to our bashful young ingénude that, come hell or high water, her boss-cum-mistress was not one to take no for an answer. Never in a thousand years, in fact, would it ever be conceivable for such a phenomenon to come to pass (not even in one's least pragmatic utopian fantasies), for, when all is dead and gone, 'twas against the foundational principles of all seven branches of physics, as regards Celine Dreadmiller's mercurial temperament, that she would ever make concessions unfavorable to her own immediate ends. And, at this point in time, she was irrevocably fixated upon punishing Yvette for her monstrously flagrant immorality.

At her boss's intimation of the grim prospect of being publicly mocked and ridiculed, Yvette felt a warm rush of blood surging through her veins, which conduced towards the sly insinuendo, imparted from the cluttered and disorganized junkyard of her id through her hyper-inflated ego to her tyrannically oppressive superego, if only in the darkest recesses of her subconscious, that there was a secret part of her soul someplace or other that relished unreservedly the counter-intuitive, seemingly non-subversive idea of people in positions of power & authority making momentous decisions in her own behalf without consulting her beforehand, telling her what to do and what not to do, and so on, even if it meant she would have no choice but to sacrifice every last vestige of her sartorial dignity and psychosexual autonomy to reach an exalted condition in which she wouldn't have any more anxieties or responsibilities to speak of: a state of mind, heart, and spirit that would (at least in some measure) nullify the unspeakable terror of her day-to-day earthbound existence or, more simply put, ensure a controlled regression back to the womb.

"I-I-I also haven't been feeling very well lately," she whimpered with downcast eyes in a last-ditch effort to gain a modicum of sympathy from her employer.

"Oh no, you poor wittle baby!"cooed Celine with a pinch of salt in her voice, "you haven't been feelin' well lately? Well, butter my butt and call me a biscuit! I'm so, *so,* very, *very* sorry to hear that!"

Celine then thrust herself towards our heroine with an exaggerated show of mock solicitude, and placed her palm over Yvette's sinciput to ascertain whether or not it felt unduly clammy or feverish. "Did you hear what she said, men? Li'l Evie here sez she ain't feelin' so good."

The delivery serviceman, Dr. Dweebaldo van Boofus, and President Ulrich Armstrong all made a show of commiserating with Yvette by performing a collective facial nuance of ersatz sympathy, whereupon they, too, thrust themselves deep into our subdebutante's discomfort zone to give her compassionate pats on her bare shoulders and knees, which made her squirm with the jitters.

"Hmmm, let's find out if you're running a temperature, shall we?" suggested Celine, who, with her quick eyes, had already spotted the rectal thermometer on the dresser. "Dr. Van Boofus, would you be so kind as to escort this young lady to her futon and have her lie belly down upon it so we can get a better idea of how truly sickified she is? That way we can make an informed determination as to whether or not it'll be necessary to call in a doctor from the station house to give her a full medical examination from head to foot, inside and out."

Yvette recomembered, to her chagrin, that one of the perks of her job was its high-quality health care, which included free visits, at the drop of a hat, from a licensed proctologist and/or obstetrician gynecologist whensoe'er an in-depth physical examination was esteemed exigent.

"No problem, ma'am," replied Dr. Van Boofus as he approached our mortified subdebutante, who was cowering at her work desk, blushingly shame-faced, petrified with trepidation, and sheepishly atremble with a notably bad case of the jimjams. Without further ado, Dweebaldo Van Boofus hoisted her up from her chair with both of his sinewy arms and escorted her by the ear (as one would a badly behaved child) to the stripped leather futon in her bedchamber. Because she put up a modicum of resistance to being manhandled by him in this way, Dr. Van Boofus smacked her thrice smartly on the fleshy part of her thigh with the singular purpose of making it abundantly clear to her Spoilt Majesty, for her own sake and benefit if no one else's, the portentous ponderance of perstanding, beyond the shadow of any doubt whatsoever, the imperative compushency of acknowledging explicitly (by virtue of her attitude, comportment, and personal demeanor), who, in point of fact, was at the helm, the which minor reprimand wound up being all the wakeup call necessitated to ensure her meek and humble compliance from that point forward, howsoever sullenly & resentfully it might appear to have been effectualized, what with our dashed subdebutante's cute pouty-lipped facial expressions and whatnot, to a fly on the wall in her sleeping chamber.

Dr. Van Boofus commanded Yvette to recline procumbently in such manner as to permit her groin area, betwixt her umbilical cord remnant and the fork of her crotch, to rest snugly atop of a portable bumper-boosting platform, known in the vernacular as an "anal pedestal," made out of chopped strand mats of fiberglass coated with silicone rubber, that had been placed upon the croc leather futon by Professor Armstrong for the purpose of enabling our heroine's pert young bottom-cheeks to be sufficiently elevated and outspread to reveal the distended opening to her cackpipe, which our discomfited subdebutante apprehended (without any need for additional persuasive measures to be implemented) she had no choice but to obey, howsoever fearfully & tearfully. Quivering with agonizing suspense, her mouth agape with incredulity as she watched her boss applying a massive glob of mentholated lubricant to a six-inch long rectal thermometer, Yvette felt her pulse quicken and her breath rate increase. Before our distraught coquette could utter so much as a peep of protest, the thermometer was intromitted gently but firmly deep inside the darkest penetralian recesses of her rectal cavity. She had never felt so utterly mortified in all her life, which was exacerbated all the more by the radiating heat of the mentholated unguent doing its dirty business inside her anal canal.

"I'm afraid," warned Celine, "that this is one of those old-fashioned thermometers that takes anywhere from ten to fifteen minutes to register an accurate reading. In the event that we discover you have a fever, we'll call in a licensed sexual physician from the precinct to come over here to examine you thoroughly—and I mean *thoroughly*—catch? If your temperature turns out to be normal, as I expect it will, then you'll be summarily spanked by one of my servicemen and evicted from these premises in double-quick time. *Farshteyst?*"

Before Yvette had a chance to respond, Celine shifted her attention back to the three alpha males in the room who had been watching our heroine's grueling ordeal unfold with what her seasoned girlish instincts informed her was a heightened concupiscent fascination.

"Gentlemen," said Celine, "as you can quite plainly see, our little notch-girl here is all bashful and nervous and fidgety and all. I mean, just look at how she keeps wriggling around on the mattress like a little earthworm! Would you be so kind as to lend me a helping hand by holding her down firmly by her floppers & benders so that she'll remain still? It's really more for her own safety than for our subjective gratification, especially as it's important to take care that the temp stick doesn't break inside her butthole. The very last thing we need right now is to be sued for mercury poisoning—banish the thought!

"Incidentally, I want to say that I feel dutifully obliged to offer all three of you fine gentlemen my profoundest apologies for this young lady's unspeakably atrocious manners, disrespectful attitude, and abominably vile behavior. As you can see for yourselves, she's quite an uncultured, uncouth, and uncivilized little creature. If

I'd had even the faintest inkling in advance that she was possessed of such poor character, I would never have dreamt of hiring her in the first place."

Professor Ulrich Armstrong, Dr. Dweebaldo Van Boofus, and the delivery serviceman did their absolute utmost, in a concerted effort to go to the greatest of all possible lengths, to reassure Fräulein Dreadmiller that the willfully egregious misconduct of this particular warehouse employee was in no wise her fault—not by a long chalk. They expressed to her their heartfelt convictions that she oughtn't to ride so roughshod over herself, as 'twas patently obvious to each and every one of them that Celine's recalcitrant employee harbored some gravely serious psycho-nymphomaniacal issues that could only be addressed efficaciously with a competently administered, no-nonsense disciplinary regimen of old-school aversion therapy.

Moved by their comforting reassurances that she shouldn't feel obliged to stand the blunt for her mercenary hireling's paughty and impertinent demeanor, Celine Dreadmiller dropped a humble curtsy and shed a tear of affectionate gratitude for their vote of confidence in her behalf.

Dr. Van Boofus grabbed both of Yvette's arms whilst Professor Armstrong and the delivery serviceman gripped her firmly by her dexter and sinistral pedestrian digits so as to keep her from dancing upon them with the sharp points of her high-heeled stilettos. Our flustered young heroine knew that she had no choice now but to submit to this degrading treatment without objection. Whilst her tormentors waited avidly for the clinical thermometer to register a precise reading, Yvette caught her breath and summoned within herself just enough by way of unblushing audacity to beg her boss to call her brother Eiden on her cellphone to ask him to return her bag of laundry so that she could put her clothes on in advance of vacating the premises.

"That's not my concern, sweetie," replied Celine. "If we determine that you're not unwell, I'll want you to pack your bags and get the hell outta here by 1:00 o'clock sharp, *verstehst du mich?* That oughta give you time aplenty to sort out your affairs and be gone from here for good and all. Should you, for any reason whatsoever, refuse to accept my offer to allow you to vacate these premises of your own volition, I'll have no choice but to call in security to escort you to the curb, for I sincerely regret to inform you that, as of this very instant, you are hereby officially dismissed from your post! Have I made myself clear?"

"Please, ma'am," Yvette pleaded, "Eiden took my clothes to the dry cleaners to have them laundered. I can't leave my apartment until I get them back so I can make myself decent in public."

"Oh boo-hoo-hoo!" scoffed Celine, "you're such a spoilt little crybaby! 'Decent,' thou sayest? That's risible! Just look at yerself, honey! You're anything but that. In fact, 'decent' is the very last modifier I would use to characterize the kind of human being you are." There were unanimous grunts of agreement from the three men surrounding her.

"You know what, girl?" continued Celine. "Your attitude is really beginning to grate on my nerves. I've been incredibly lenient with you up to this point. But I must say, your whole mental make-up of moral entitlement really gets my dander up. There are few things that peeve me more than worthless individuals, who prove themselves time and again to be naught but shiftless ne'er-do-wells, who think and act as though they deserve exclusive privileges and preferential treatments over those who are infinitely more creditable and accomplished than they could ever imagine themselves to be in their wildest dreams. 'Tis precisely that kinda thing that irks me no end. People who act all high & mighty, when there's nothin' soever in their attainments to merit so much as even a whit of such bigheadedness, really set my teeth on edge. Bear's asses in genius's clothing; affectatious artistes without any craft or skill; la-de-dah, status-seeking, social-climbing morons who have the temerity to comment on chaotic world affairs, as if they were above it all, whilst partaking of unconscionably extortionate high tea services every shank of the afternoon, week after week, in their zillionaire country clubs, who are themselves naught but know-it-all know-nothings—such people get under my skin like you wouldn't believe! If afforded the opportunity, I'd take each an' every last one o' them off the calendar by tooth, fang, an' claw! I'd gauge out their eyes with a red-hot pruning fork and feed them to a sharp-set float of man-eating saltwater crocodiles! I'd thrust them feet foremost into a woodchipper! I'd roll them starbolic through a field of stinging nettles, then boil them alive in a cauldron of liquid asphalt! I'd vivisect them inch by inch and flush each chunk of their raw flesh down a domestic garbage grinding unit whilst making abso-pharking-lutely sure as eggs is eggs that their neurological systems would be kept on high alert and their optics held wide open (assisted, of course, by state-of-the-art, Clockwork-Orange-style ophthalmic specula) to guarantee they would witness (with blind, panic-struck expressions on their phizogs) every last gory little detail of their dying moments on Mother Earth! Are you focused on what I'm sayin'...?"

Truth be told, Yvette Cartier was listening to Celine's vituperative harangue with the ultra-super-hyper-attentive vigilance of a goatish Peeping Tom in quixotic quest of catching sight of an exposed love point, frightened out of her wits as to what it foretokened in terms of the maze of nightmares that lay in store for her, as she could not help but draw the terrifying inference that Celine's thunderous jeremiad was a pre-calculated tongue-lashing that was deliberately and single-mindedly being levied against her and no one else in particular. Our shamefaced ingénude could not forgo arriving at the pessimistic conclusion that these reproachful upbraidings from her ex-boss were meant to function as a full-frontal assault on her ethico-moral integrity. Unable to set up an effective line of defense against Ms. Dreadmiller's destructive tsunami of scurrilous billingsgate, our heroine could do naught but taste the heat-drops of her own profuse lachrymations as they flowed from her cheeks in small rivulets across the stripped leather futon and, undeterred by the gravitation principle, through the sweet line betwixt her naked jabongoes towards her altar of love.

"And what's so tragic and depressing about such phenomena," continued Celine, "is that they are by no means unwont to being encountered high and low throughout the land, pervasive as skunks in their dens and rats in their burrows. We live in a schmociety whose mainstream culture gleefully glorifies intellectual destitution, moral bankruptcy, and spiritual depravity on all fronts far and wide. Our frivolization has devolved, over a few short decenniums, from an embryonic meritocracy into an all-inclusive mediocracy, and withal from a high-minded literocracy into a brute idiocracy.

"Neither my brother nor I have ever pleaded with anyone for special favors, as you yourself appear to be doing at this very moment with all your queruling, sniveling, and blubbering, like a self-important prima dollarina, that you haven't got your laundry back from the cleaners, blah-blah-blah, like it was Eiden's fault or something. Do you have any idea how expensive it is to dry-clean the hundreds of fancy-schmancy designer clothes he uncovered from your wardrobe? Your diaphanous unmentionables alone are made of such delicate and exotic fabrics that it takes professionals more than just a few days to process them. The dry-cleaning authorities even warned Eiden, long in advance, that they would be up all through the wee hours of many a morn to get the job done good & proper (wind and weather permitting, of course)—with no guarantees whatsoever that the job would get completed on time, let alone at all. You should surrealize that many of the employees at the dry-cleaning facility had to pay double-time for child-care in an effort to get the task executed in a timely manner for the sake of her Spoilt Majesty. The gentleman running the dry-cleaning service told my brother Eiden, in no uncertain terms, that he would have no choice but to hire extra temp helpers to expedite your (frankly) fredicularious order. Morefurther, many of the temps, the thumping majority of whom are restive and rebellious on miscount of being paid a mere pittance for their tedious and backbreaking work—which mandates tightening security on and around the site of the dry-cleaning facility (a by no means inconsiderable cost in and of itself)—were called in by their agents at the Pleasant Peasant Corporation in the weest hours of the night to lend their helping hands in the all but vain hopes of bringing your order to successful fruition by its arbitrary deadline. My dear brother Eiden, out of the goodness of his heart, bent over backwards to accommodate your frivolous needs and then just listen to yourself, like an entitled little drama queen with all that griping and groaning and kvetching and bitching and yammering and whatnot! You probably didn't even realize that Eiden had to work late shifts every single night for the past six weeks scrubbing toilets—in maximum-security prisons, no less—just so he could afford to pay your fucking laundry bill! So the very least thing you could do is show him some gratitude, thou unthankful, sniveling, grumblesome, whiny little bitch!"

Yvette was grievously mortified to hear all of this, which was only compounded by the fact that she was being held firmly in place, flat on her stomach, by three virile middle-aged manly types, with her unshielded Brazilian-waxed crotch resting upon the anal pedestal that had been placed atop of the stripped leather futon by the dean and president of her school whilst having her already acute discomfiture intensified by virtue of there being a ginormous rectal thermometer waving its loud flag from deep inside her rectum, and all of this in the course of being harshly scolded by her lover's stunningly gorgeous older sister, whom our red-faced sub-debutante held in the highest imaginable dainty due to her amazingly impressive worldwide connections in the fashion industry.

"Both of us," continued Celine, "had to work from the ground up and learn things the hard way from square one, without access to any resources to speak of. From the day we were born we had to pay our parents retroactively for all our food, clothing, and shelter. And we're still paying off our parental loans. I was actually inclined to vouchsafe thee the benefit of the doubt by permitting you to abnegate this abode in peace, unencumbered by the bureaucrappic inconveniences that would inevitably emerge in the process of leveling significant charges against thee, but now, seeing as how brazenly impudent thou art, I must admit that I'm beginning to have some serious second thoughts about letting you go scot-free. I'm accrescently inclined, in fact, to review my position on this matter. A mild admonition—a remedial lesson in the social codes and graces—may not be amiss under the circumstances. If you had read the fine print of the contract you had signed, with the indefatigable due diligence I expect from each and every one of my employees, you would have successively become apprised of the fact (which I had gone to the trouble of taking great pains to make a point of highlighting multiple times in second-coming type, using red fluorescent ink, no less) that, aside from having no free perks on any of the merchandise in the adjoining warehouse, not only because inventory is incredibly tight and profit margins virtually negligible, you are also forbidden, in no 'unsquirtin' sperms,'—and don't you dare groan at my pun or I'll put thee in stocks and cane thy naked arse and have thee tarred and feathered from tit to toe in the town square, thou slimy little slutch!—from pettin' yer pussycat on the premises, which, by the bye, makes for singularly poor public relations, whether you're caught in flagrante delicto or no, and for which the punishment is exceptionally severe, as expressly delineated in both the fine print and flaring second-coming type of the contract you had so cavalierly neglected to read before signing, most likely due to the flippantly fallacious assumption you were conditioned by the milieu created by the stinkin' filthy nouveau-riche beau monde in which you were coddlingly bred to nurture, that the system, in and of itself, is, to the very end of the chapter, acquiescent only to your lusts and longings and no one else's, and, moreover, only when the cows give beer (which, of course, will never happen in a thousand millennia, from your credit group's perspective), the science-fictional reversal of fortune (an alternative universal other-way-aroundness of a kind) would be vaguely foreseeable to fetch itself up in the offing. In any case, I really don't think you wanna go down that alley now, d'ya, girlie...?"

A tiny bell rang on the rectal thermometer accompanied by a nursery tune, indicating that an accurate reading of Yvette's temperature had been recorded. It had taken at least twice the amount of time than her ex-boss had estimated it would. Celine yanked the thermometer out of Yvette's anus and tisk-tisked upon reading it. "Good news and bad news, sweetie. Your temperature is 98.6 degrees Fahrenheit, which is normal, so there's nothing really serious that's ailing you. The bad news is that there are strict consequences for feigning illness. To approach this matter open-mindedly, however, I am by no means disinclined to conjecture that the symptoms you are manifesting are a psychosomatically induced response to the physical stress of your laborious new occupation, compounded tenfold by the immense multitude of inordinately long work shifts you have been obliged to ensuffer here, you poor wretched little creature, you." Celine paused for effect, stroking the back of Yvette's lap gently in a mock effort to console her and, in the course of so doing, drawing stifled yet audible titters from the three gents holding her down by her arms and legs. "I think this pathetic little attempt on your part at feigning illness is merely a delay tactic to postpone your upcoming compendium of corrective sanctions."

At Celine's mention of the terrifying prospect of being subjugated to "sanctions" (pluralized) rather than a sanction (singular), Yvette felt a wasabi-like sting of warmth radiating from her rectal cavity, evidently caused by the mentholated lubricant Celine had applied to the thermometer. The juxtaposition of its calidity with the chilly air circulating around her apartment made our heroine feel inordinately oomphy, both inside and out. It was all she could do to avoid erupting with a stupendous orgasm in front of the four individuals assembled around her, the very thought of which gave her the squirms. She prayed fervently to Jesus that they wouldn't notice her pussy was getting all moist and clammy inside in response to the unexpected thrill she was experiencing from being scolded and disciplined.

"Before we evict you from these premises," continued Celine, "the honorable dean & president of Pimpleton State Luniversity would like to have a brisk word with you. Would you like us to leave the room, Ulrich?"

"No, no, that won't be necessary, Celine, now that the brat's outta the bag." Professor Armstrong placed both of his hands on Yvette's nude backside and took five or six minutes to gently yet firmly rub her flush young nether cheeks down with a vast spectrum of glistening lubricants she had stolen from the warehouse, until both of her buns had developed a luminously oleaginous shine to them, which made our bash ingénude feel phenomenally venereous.

"Mademoiselle Cartier," said Professor Armstrong, "I came here with glad tidings regarding the latest updates on your academic future but have just now been presented with some hard and incriminating evidence, nay, incontestable proof even, from Dr. Dweebaldo Van Boofus here, of your fraudulent academic conduct. This, of course, changes everything. You were about to be awarded a full scholarship for the duration of your years (and retroactively as well for time served) as an undergraduate student at our college, which would have included all tuition expenses, free room and board, and a generous research stipend into the bargain (not to mention a pecuniary bonus that would have enabled you to make a four-fifths downpayment on a seven-bedroom luxury lakefront home right here in Pimpleton Heights). Now that the tables have been turned 180 degrees, however, we have no recourse at this point in time but to take stern and exacting corrective disciplinary measures against thee."

The president and dean of Pimpleton State Luniversity, who spoke with a deep basso profondo, lending to his vox the kind of commanding authoricratic complexion that was seld if ever challenged by anybody or their in-laws, was nearly thrice Yvette's age and at least three heads taller than she was, which made the close proximity of his physical presence formidably menacing (and amorously intoxicating as well, she thought). He held up a strong and powerful hand that looked as though it could span upwards of two octaves on a keyboard and made a forceful swinging gesture therewith, as if to test the currents of cold air that were blasting down from the vents in the ceiling, which conveyed unambiguously to our shy young ingénude his imminent intent.

Psychologically unprepared, albeit palpitating anticipatorily, for what Professor Armstrong was about to do to her blait young blind-cheeks, which were withal conveniently elevated upon the anal pedestal atop of the croc leather futon in her boudoir, Yvette Cartier squeaked timorously, "Please don't, sir!" at which point she felt an unconstrained consecution of smart skelps on her naked catastrophe. And, unlike the little love taps Eiden had administered upon her in their childish little role-playing rituals, these smacks were hard and hot and astonishingly painful.

"Ow!" she yelped, beside herself with barefaced confusion and shame. "That hurts!" In the words of Leopold Bloom, in the Circe episode of Ulysses, she felt a "warm tingling glow without effusion."

"Of course it hurts, you brazen little hussy!" rejoined the dean impatiently. "You have brought shame and disgrace upon the venerable institution I administrate and, by extension, a stain upon mine own reputation as its chief arbiter and representative. What do you think I'm going to say now to the generous, kindhearted benefactors on the scholarship subcommittee who have flown halfway across the country—on a violently turbulent flight, I might add—to attend the ceremony honoring you and your allegedly 'outstanding scholarly achievements' tomorrow evening at six o'clock sharp...? What possible bloody excuse can I give them...? At least three members of the subcommittee were forced to cancel their pre-paid quinquennial holiday vacations that had been planned for years (if not decades) in advance that would have been spent with members of their extended families, including several distant relatives who had themselves saved money for years, if not decades, so they, too, could afford to fly in from far abroad to meet them in the Emirate of Dubai for this special reunion for the first time in over thirty years and what may very well end up being their final chance to see one another face to face and catch up since old times spent together in the distant past on an East African safari. Another two members of the subcommittee were already under hospice care, given only two weeks and three months, respectively, to make their final arrangements. Out of the goodness of their hearts (bless theirs souls!) they felt duty-bound to muster whatever strength and energy they still had within them, even to the point of forgoing their thrice-weekly hemodialysis treatments, to attend this special celebration in your behalf. Five of the other subcommittee members cancelled their hard-earned, long-planned holiday cruises on the Caribbean, the Mediterranean, to the Galápagos Islands for wildlife viewing, to Northern Antarctica to walk with the penguins, and the Panama Canal to take pictures of monkeys with their friends and families only for your sake—not theirs—as they were worried this celebration would be ill-attended and that your feelings might be hurt if they weren't there to give you their full and unconditional moral support. As it is, all twelve members of this venerable subcommittee have already been booked in five-star hotel suites (mostly at their own expense and only partly from matching financial donations squeezed out of funds raised by the regents of Pimpleton State and at least a dozen other prestigious institutions of higher earning, not to mention a handful of in-kind grants from local psychiatrists and pain therapists to supply the cupcakes and cookies at your reception) eagerly working into the weest hours of the morning for the past several months, relying solely on energy drinks to keep themselves awake and alert, making preparations for this grand ceremonious occasion in your so-called 'honor!'"

The dean & president, who had worked himself up into a phrenzy, grabbed our heroine roughly and laid her face-down over his lap, whereupon he administered more punitive smackings on her pert young bottom than she was able to count, and briskly enough to redden her buns for weeks, if not months, thereafter. And, to make matters exponentially more humiliating, Celine Dreadmiller, Dweebaldo Van Boofus, and the delivery serviceman (the latter of whom was a complete stranger to Yvette, notwithstanding that she found him cute in a teddy-bearish cuddly sort of way) watched this toe-curling spectacle with bated breath, as it unfolded before their enraptured eyes, with expressions of proud satisfaction on their phizogs.

Okay, she thought, sobbing with bitter remorse. They had driven their point home. Perhaps they would now rest assured that she had learnt her lesson, and learnt it soundly, for she knew in her heart of hearts that she would never so much as even entertain the foggiest fanciable notion, much less the remotest imaginable inkling, of ever embarking upon the multi-dimensionally convoluted maneuvers of taking it upon herself to countenance the faintest potentiality of giving the most infinitesimal iota of the briefest deliberation over the by no manner of means un-scarce verisimility that she would at any time in the near, never mind the remote, foreseeable future focus so much as even the minutest percentage of her metaphysical contemplations upon the immeasurably distant prospect of finding herself in a negligibly favorable position to consider the slightest ghost of a chance of taking advantage of the most minuscule conceivable window of opportunity to ever steal or cheat again as long as she lived, so help her God, amen! It simply wasn't worth the trouble after everything they had just put her through.

After President & Dean Ulrich Armstrong had finished lambasting our extraught young coquette on her uncovered posterior, she was granted a few moments to re-generate herself from this over-stimulation of her circulation by being forcibly laid upon the cool leather futon, sprawled out on her stomach with her lady parts in-decently exposed, so she could reflect upon her dire misdoings whilst Celine gently applied a scented salve to the crimson marks of shame on her cooler. Incompatible with her current predicament, Yvette felt confident—howsoever delusionally—that, at any moment now, Eiden Dreadmiller, her imaginary knight in shining armor, would arrive there to rescue her, and that she would ere long be vouchsafed the suffrage to walk out of there, dressed to impress (as was normal for her), and that, although she would feel sorely contrite from having been so sternly reprimanded, she would still be able to make her departure in grace and in one piece, and at very least with an outward semblance of her erstwhile dignity in tact, howsoever improbable such a scenario might seem under the present about-standings.

Now that her baptism of fire was at long last drawing to a close, she breathed a sigh of relief that it hadn't transpired in a public setting (heaven forfend!), as she had briefly misdoubted it might, judging from the undercurrent of intimations that such a horrorshow would likely be the case in the inflections and modulations of Celine's cruel-hearted utterances. Yvette figured that if she had to take remedial courses at the local community college to make up for her academic defallations, then so be it. She would do whatever was necessary to compensate for lost time and wasted tuition expenses. She would even consider going so far as to confess all her mortal and venial sins to a Holy Roman inquisitor, if need be. Having recollected chapter 10, verse 9 in Proverbs that reads, "He that walketh uprightly walketh surely: But he that perverteth his ways shall be known," she felt a newfound confidence that, now that her wily ways had been exposed and her sins and transgressions had been fully expiated by Celine's harsh scoldings and President Armstrong's punitive sconings, she felt ripe and ready to "walk securely in integrity," as she sensed was her present calling.

Her soft-boiling, slow-simmering ruminations were interrupted, seeming out of the blue, by the telephone ringing at full volume in the adjoining office. Startled by the sound, Yvette stood up instinctively to go answer it, albeit barely a second after Celine had already beaten her to the punch.

"Eiden, good to hear from you … No, she's leaving right now as we speak. I have an errand for her to do for me … Sure, Eiden, meet me at Mildred's next door and bring Francine along if you like. Oh…? She's already on the way…? Is she bringing the entire tech crew with her…? Excellent! I'll be there in about twenty minutes, if not sooner … Okay, love you too, bro! See you there! Bye-bye!"

Yvette's heart sank when she surrealized that her ex-boss had forgotten to ask Eiden to bring her clean laundry back to her apartment. She felt an overpowering urge to speak up, as there was no way in hell she was ever going to vacate the premises with nary a stitch to her name, especially now that the swamping shame of her humiliation experience would be compounded a thousandfold by the hot red marks of disrepute on her sky-clad duff were it to be seen by any souls outside her apartment (assuming, of course, that these four consummate professionals, who had just gone to the trouble of teaching her a strict lesson through the instrumentality of their seasoned disciplinary methods, obeyed the time-honored corporate ethics policy that, quote, "this does not leave the room," unquote). If word ever got out regarding the tokens of shame on her nether regions, she would betimes devolve into the town jesting-stock once the local tongue-wagging machine got into full gear, which was right-down unthinkable, for such a pudendous spectacle as she was now fancifying could ne'er in a thousand years betide her Spoilt Majesty—most-wise in a public setting in front of an unruly crowd of randy spectators. 'Twas quite plain and simply impossimaginable! Or so her deeply ingrained normalcy bias (which caused her to minimize in her mind's eye virtually every threat warning in plain sight of her person, as well as to underestimate the probable impacts and repercussions of impending disastrophes, should they eventuate) had convinced her.

In an unplunge there sounded a brisk business-like rap on the front door of her apartment followed by a sudden draught of fresh cold air filling the room. "Ah, Francine, so glad you could make it," said Celine, as she opened the door wide to admit six newcomers into Yvette's apartment. "I was just on the phone with Eiden. You're here much earlier than I expected. I guess the traffic must've been light, huh? Come right in!"

Our anxious ingénude felt grievously disconcerted at the prospect of being sighted in her present undignified state by yet another group of random individuals, not only for being in her native buff per se (with no recourse whatsoever but to remain thuswise until her rags were safely returned) but even more so for the scarlet letter of infamy that was now lucently glowing on her seat of shame, aggravated by the fact that these people (complete strangers to her, on the face of it) would be able to espy this emblem of her ignominy, in all its grandeur and obloquy, even though she herself would ne'er be granted the selfsame opportunity, owing to its out-of-the-way whereabouts on her back-parts. For aught she knew, these striped burning logos of disgrace on her fundamental features could very well be conspicuously more pronounced in magnitude than she had originally conjectured, based on how rough and craggy they felt when she stroked them with the bare palms of her hands.

A stunningly attractive, severe looking young blonde woman in a bespoke, tailored, high-powered business suit, who looked vaguely familiar to Yvette, entered the apartment with a crisply uniformed tech crew consisting of five athletic looking young men carrying pocket-size tool kits who immediately went about the premises disassembling surveillance gear that Yvette had never even noticed before. The gear consisted of a host of hidden video cameras and listening devices of seeming nanometric dimensions that were virtually invisible to the naked eye. The fact that these people didn't so much as even bat an eye upon catching our discomposed heroine stripped to the buff and in an awkward procumbent position atop of an anal pedestal on the futon, as she now was, did nothing to allay her acute paranoia as to what prezactly these people were doing inside her apartment. Without warning, two masty members of the tech crew, at the direction of the young woman called Francine, lifted Yvette off the futon's anal pedestal by her arms & legs, copping a feel or two here and there to ensure her enhanced cooperation, and then laid her down, flat on her back, on the dormeuse chaise lounge in the living room so that they could proceed unencumbered with disengaging dozens of hidden surveillance devices (mostly cameras & microphones) that had been deeply embedded in, on, and around the croc leather futon.

It would be no exaggeration to say that Yvette was strung out and packed tight by what she was witnessing, especially upon the nigh instantaneous surrealization that she recognized the young woman called Francine from the "Big-Sister-is-Watching-You" mug shot she had seen hanging in Helga Armstrong's office at the campus administration building on Thursday last, exactly one week ago to the hour.

CHAPTER TWELVE

"W hat—?" exclaimed Celine in mock-surprise when she encountered Yvette cowering in a fetal position on the chaise longue. "You're still here? I can't *believe* it! I thought you'd left hours ago. It's well past 1:00 o'clock!"

In one fell swoop Celine yanked Yvette down into a doggy-style position on the floor and gave her a sound smacking on her sit-me-down, which not only stung her smartly but was especially mortifying for her in the direct presence of Professor Armstrong's daughter and her tech crew, each and every member of whom were casting her sidelong po-faced glances interspersed with old-fashioned mussitations of rufty-tufties, not to mention the three other male individuals, who had, among-hands, made themselves cosily comfy at her dining-room set, snug as bugs in a rug, with a hearty repast from a mouth-watering array of sumptuous deli items they'd purloined from Yvette's $42,000.00 Meneghini La Cambusa frigidaire, including a $6,000.00 bottle of Domaine Leflaive Chevalier-Montrachet Grand Cru white wine from Burgundy, which our squelched young coquette had been saving for a special occasion.

The entry bell rang and Celine immediately opened the front door to admit into Yvette's living quarters (without asking her permission to do so) a tall, thick-set, broad-shouldered man in cargo pants and a uniform shirt bearing the name and logo of a regional locksmith company. He handed his calling card to Celine and immediately got to work changing the pins and springs inside the lock assembly of the front door to Yvette's apartment. As he did this, he kept stealing lecherous up-and-downs and thrice-overs at our timid young ingénue with the apprehensive, half-starved demeanor of one who has seld if ever laid eyes on a beautiful young demi-vierge in the buff before, which, while she found such psychosexual vulnerability touching (especially when exuded from such a big macho he-man as this locksmith indubitably was), caused Yvette all the same to feel excruciatingly uncomfortable and self-conscious in his presence. The beads of sweat running down the man's furrowed sinciput were palpable, to say the least, and were matched, in part, by the clammy moisture in Yvette's vajayjay, indicating to her that, in all likelihood, the locksmith's musky scent was arousing her more than she would ever be willing to admit. To make matters worse—much worse—the presence of this stranger and ten others in her apartment did nothing whatsoever to deter our heroine's ex-boss from propelling onward in a loud incisive voice with her denunciatory invective, tirades of abuse, and ominous threats (seeming without end) of implementing stern corrective disciplinary measures on the priviest regions of our heroine's exposed anatomy in recompense for her suppositious insubordination, obstinate disobedience, and intemperate nymphomaniacal proclivities. Of course, it goes without saying that this extraordinary callousness on the part of her ex-boss, insofar as she demonstrated no conscientious ethico-moral qualms whatsoever about openly discussing private and sensitive matters—more appropriately discussed behind closed doors in the offices of trained psychotherapists (or what are more colloquially known as "Psycho the Rapists")—appertaining to Yvette's problematic predilection for compulsive self-gratification, namely: her apparent pathological addiction to all-night wrist marathons, excessive five-knuckle-shuffles, and other modes of perverted behavior, including her patently conspectable propensity for brazen exhibitionism (to which all parties present could now give first-hand eyewitness testimony if called upon to do so by the judicial authorities), her unrestrained sexual hedonism (as incontrovertibly proven by hordes of direct, circumstantial, testimonial, and forensic evidence not only in the glaringly egregious fact of Yvette's shocking and shameless nudity on & off the job but also in the highly suggestive corroborating indicators thereof by the hundreds of open bottles of aphrodisiacal lubricants, love & pleasure toys, physical restraints such as ankle bracelets & handcuffs, portable powered devices designed for sexual penetration and what have you scattered helter-skelter all over her apartment) in front of a complete stranger (the locksmith) who had obviously taken a lubricious shine to Yvette, not to mention all the others going about their business inside her apartment who were well within earshot of Celine's venomously savage vituperations, did nothing whatsoever to alleviate our heroine's primordial sentiments of abject shame and humiliation at being dressed down by her ex-boss in front of everyone and their in-laws.

Yvette's gravest concern at the moment was that Celine Dreadmiller might get it into her ruthless mindset to punish her even more severely by granting this big horny locksmith free rein to have his way with her howsoever he saw fit. 'Twas enormously challenging for our petite young ingénude to imagine how this cockstrong man, who was almost seven feet tall and proportionally wide of girth, could fit his engorged member (which, judging from the expanding protrusion in his combat trousers, was massively prodigious in size) inside her tight little jing-jang, were things ever to devolve into such a grim scenario, which she sorely hoped they wouldn't (at least, based upon an antediluvian set of principles she had heretofore talked herself into fervently embracing for the nonce).

"Well, as it turns out," said Celine, "I've decided to be lenient with you by holding off for now on calling in security to escort you to the curb. Instead, whether you like it or lump it, I'm going to chaperone you myself next door to Mildred's Market, which is run and owned by my dad, Justyce Dreadmiller. He told me, in no uncertain terms (and in thine own case, sweetie, 'no unhurtin' squirms,' bwa-ha-ha!), that he'd like to have a special word with thee: hardball to eyeball. He said it had something to do with his long-standing compunction of conscience as concerns what he felt was his ethical imperative to enlighten thee in the propers & fine points, as well as the punctilios & particulars, in conjunction with the myriad jots and tittles of certain rudimental moral precepts appertaining to thine observed malefacts and thick-spinnings (all of which have been meticulously videographed by Professor Armstrong's bright young daughter here, who, as you may have surmised, is an up-and-coming surveillance engineer par excellence) within the last two and a half years of your perseening to patronize his business in the hopes that his recommendations for enhancement would serve to disabuse you of whatsoever preconceived notions you may have nurtured apropos of the manner in which to decorously conduct thyself whilst setting foot on the grounds of his venerable establishment."

Yvette realized then and there that she had failed to connect the name Mildred with Dreadmiller, for she had hithertowards been unaware that the store from which she had routinely purloined cosmetics and love toys was owned and managed by Eiden & Celine's father—a man whom, in the last few days, she had crossed her fingers would eventually become her father-in-law once she had tied the connubial knots with his son. Suffice it to say, these were by no manner of means the mode of farcosts wherein she had envisioned herself being formally introduced to her presumptive future father-in-law.

Without warning, a jet of ice-cold water hit Yvette's privy-hole and midriff, catching her completely unawares. It seemed to come out of nowhere until our heroine surrealized it was from an automated squirt gun with a long range high pressure capacity that Celine had removed from one of the packages of sex toys used by sadists for hosing down submissives—a device that Yvette vaguely reco-membered having boosted from the shelves of the warehouse a day or two before. It was also favored by pet owners for discouraging dogs and cats from jumping onto kitchen tables and countertops.

Our heroine could not help but take note that the locksmith was still leering at her with an unyieldingly stony expression on his dial, tinged with anxiety, that could only be construed (unless she'd been born on a different planet) to signify an unslakable hankering on his part to buckle her down and bone her hard and fast on the spot. However that may be, what disturbed her even more than this man's unchecked lewd and suggestive behavior, through the medium of his off-color facial mannerisms, was that Celine Dreadmiller, who had just appointed herself to act as Yvette's unofficial chaperone, catching on to the locksmith's unseemly fascination with her charge, gave the man what appeared to be an encouraging, almost conspiratorial, look (akin to a crocodile grin) accompanied by a subtle nod & wink, as if to say to him, "go for it!" Notwithstanding the burgeoning protuber-ance (a veritable cockasaurus-rex) that our groveled young ingénude took tent of that was straining the crotch seams of the keymaker's combat trousers, the manly man appeared to be at loggerheads with his conscience (if, in fact, he owned one) apropos of tacitly accepting Celine's offer, most probably indicating that he was ball-and-chained and thus, very likely, had way too much on his platter at stake to launch himself headlong into extramarital machiavellianisms. Suffice it to say, our abashed subdebutante did her darnedest not to give away any signs in her outward deportment and demeanor of the acute disappointment she felt.

"Whaddya think you're doing?" barked Celine. "Drifting off with the pixies and fairies again...? I can't believe what a mindless little airhead you are! Stop chasing rainbows and chop to it! We're leaving *now! Jetzt! Sofort!*"

Dweebaldo Van Boofus and Professor Armstrong, tipsy on the dispendious bottle of wine they'd just imbibed, yanked Yvette from her protective cowering position into an upright stance, whereupon they forcibly wrenched her arms behind her back (casting therethrough her every last vestige of pretensions to maidenly modesty out the window) and bound her wrists with the hinged Smith & Wesson hand-cuffs she'd so cavalierly left in plain sight atop of the dresser in her boudoir. Her now exposed full-frontal assets attracted, with an even greater intensity of luxurity, the unwanted attention of the locksmith, who once again gave Yvette a lecherous thrice-over whilst appearingly licking his chops in anticipation of an exquisite re-fection. The door to her apartment was opened wide and she was escorted by her mistress and masters out into the cavernous warehouse, which was even chillier than her apartment. Celine remunerated the locksmith for the new set of keys to Yvette's apartment and tipped the man generously. Thereupon she invited him to the special event next door at Mildred's Market whilst looking him directly in the eye and alternately casting meaningful sidelong glances at her handcuffed subject and, in sync thereto, raising her eyebrows thrice in quick succession and winking at the man as if to drop the hint that she would personally see to it that the party next door would be especially yum-yum for him insofar as fulfilling his most pressing aspirations. Upon vacating Yvette's apartment, Francine and her tech crew shut the door behind them and locked and bolted it tight with the new set of keys provided by the locksmith before nailing a colossal "for lease" sign onto a sandwich board next to the front entrance. The weather forecast had been for cool blustery days and frosty nights with a stiff wintry breeze off the ocean, which made it feel especially cold on the intimate parts of our heroine's anatomy that had just been douched by her ex-boss.

"Hey there! Chop chop! Make it snappy!" barked Celine at her shamefast chaper-onee. "And stop draggin' ass, you silly little girl! It's time for you to face the disso-nance and dance for us! Go on! Set the ball rollin', thou accidious, self-abusing, lazy little sluggard!" Celine shot another jet of frigid earth juice on both the small of her victim's back and the vertical groove betwixt her butt cheeks. It stung our coquette with a smartful bite for the first umpteen seconds, causing her entire body to shake like a windswept leaf on a northern plain, subsiding thereupon to a point where it felt nippy and marbly on her bare skin in the sense of serving to amplify her already acute self-consciousness at being stark-flap-naked in a semi-public space. As all twelve members of the party ascended the stairwell to the parking lot, Yvette could not help but dart quick glances around her in an all but fruitless endeavor to re-assure herself, if only transitorily, that no one had caught sight of her—at least, not yet. She could make out three or four shoppers in the distance who were loading the trunks of their cars with groceries, none of whom appeared to have noticed her being paraded through the parking lot in her natural state.

"Oh fer cripe's sake!" shouted Celine, "you're such a nervous li'l Nellie, *aintcha*? Quit bein' so floppin' antsy an' jumpy all the time! What makes ya think you're so special, anyways? As if no one's ever seen a silly, naughty little nympho like yerself bein' conferred the netted fairings of her comeuppances. Give us a friggin' break! Keep thyself still, stay calm, and be courteous to strangers if ya don't want another skelpin' on them pretty li'l flanks o' yers!"

As she was marched in handcuffs across the parking lot towards the elevator, Yvette noticed that the swollen member inside the locksmith's cargo pants had reached its full maturity, which thrilled her no end, as she could not help but feel affectionally flattered thereby. For a brief instant she was overcome by an intense desire to put this big man's little guy out of its misery by getting down on her knees to give it a sweet little mouth hug.

"Y'know what?" growled Celine, breaking Yvette's delicious reverie, "you oughtta be grateful I'm not in a less convivial mood at the moment. Otherwise I'd see to it that you're paraded on a poodle leash down Main Street all the way to Grand Central Square for a public lathering! How would ya fancy *that*, eh? Now stir them stumps, young lady, an' stop fussin' around! C'mon! Get crackin', you self-obsessed, over-precious, prissy li'l prossy!"

Dr. Dweebaldo Van Boofus pressed the floor-selection button to summon the elevator that would take them down to the ground floor, directly into the bowels of Mildred's Market. Yvette could already hear the hustle & bustle of busy shoppers going about their daily rounds on the level directly below them. She could also make out the Adagio movement of Schubert's C Major Quintet being performed by (she assumed) principal players from the local symphony orchestra (most probably the Pimpleton Philharmonic). She could not help but wonder what the festive occa-sion was that would prompt the powers that be at Mildred's to hire players of such outstanding caliber. She figured it must have been either a funeral service or a fund-raiser of sorts. She knew for a fact that players of such caliber—and the principals from the local symphony were as good as the best of the best—were neither cheap nor easy to come by, so she assumed they must have been hired many months, if not years, in advance for whatever this special occasion happened to be. When the elevator door opened to let them on, there were five individuals on it that included three freshmen boys in suit & tie she immediately recognized from one of her classes at school. Upon nailing her as well, they performed a simultaneous double-take, albeit not without opening their drooling chops out of awestruck stupefaction at having caught her in such a compromised state, especially due to the association they had heretofore developed in their collective adolescent psyches of Mademoiselle Yvette Cartier falling into the easily classifiable prototype of a super-stylish, standoffish, self-entitled, snooty little rich bitch whom they had assumed by default to be untouchable by mere mortals such as they reckoned themselves to be. They could not help but ogle her in stunned silence whilst taking in every curve of her lithe young physique with their concupiscent peepers. Yvette instinctively averted their prurient gazes, blushing crimson with humiliation, hoping they wouldn't notice that she was handcuffed or that she had loud red stripes of discredit on her naked fundament. That, however, was a tall order to expect from a trio of strapping young bucks who were, by all measures, horny as a herd of he-goats in the dog days of summer. Yvette's ex-boss-cum-chaperone, catching on to the trio's fascination with her charge, made an unambiguous "attaboy" gesture of encouragement with a nod and a wink meant to communicate to them that they were free to palp and prinkle Ms. Cartier's anatomy whithersoever and howsoever they pleased and withal to take a free tour of all the chambers in her palace of pleasure, even via the workman's entrance if they felt thus inclined, the which generous offer, of course, presuming this trio of studly young bucks was quick enough on the trigger to catch on to Celine's unambiguous solicitations in our discountenanced ingénude's bamblustercated behalf, they would be unable scientifically to turn down, driven as they were by overmastering biological impulses. As it turned out, all three members of this virile triumvirate of college-aged muscle boys took Celine up on her offer in a bang. This fearsome threesome started vigorously squeezing our heroine's supple young snorbs, stroking and goosing her tight little patoot, and gently massaging her moistening vulva to the point of causing her to have involuntary muscle contractions in her groin. Their animal caresses felt like loving gestures in comparison with the harsh spanking she had just received from the president and dean of her school. For the second or third time within the last hour or so, it was all Yvette could do to keep herself from exploding with a volcanically violent, if not brilliantly intoxicating, orgasm. Let it suffice to say that the descent down to Mildred's Market from the parking lot above was the longest single-floor vertical transportation excursion our demoralized young demigoddess had ever undertaken.

CHAPTER THIRTEEN

W hen the decorative stainless steel center-parting doors of the elevator finally opened onto the ground floor, the Schubert Adagio had just reached
its concluding perfect authentic cadence in E Major and had drawn to
a placidious close. Yvette was immediately greeted by a quintet of stern authoritative men in black suits, two or three heads taller than she was, who appeared as
though they had long been awaiting her arrival at the store. "She's all yours now,"
said Celine before strolling off into the produce section. Even though Celine had
treated Yvette with naught but the utmost contempt, our disgraced young coquette
still considered her, at this stage of the game, to be her only lifeline out of the
quagmire in which she now found herself. One of the five men stepped forward
to fasten a leather collar around Yvette's neck, evidently so that she could be led
on a leash to the proprietor of Mildred's Market. The quintet of black-suited stern
authoritative men proceeded to parade Yvette, handcuffed & collared as she was,
through the boutique's tortuous maze of aisles for several long minutes so that all
the patrons and employees could take a good gander at her gorgeous, lithe young
figure coupled with her pretty downcast eyes and plump pouty lips. Whilst she
was being modeled through the store, a vocal quintet from Italy stepped out of the
shadows to sing Carlo Gesualdo's *Moro, lasso, al mio duolo,* from his sixth book of
madrigals, published in 1611. The acoustics were superb and the singing sublime!

Moro, lasso, al mio duolo
E chi mi può dar vita,
Ahi, che m'ancide e non vuol darmi aita!

O dolorosa sorte,
Chi dar vita mi può,
Ahi, mi dà morte!

And here, for the reader, is a slightly doctored up translation of the poem from
Italian into English:

I die, wretched, of untold grief,
And the only person in the world who could save me,

Alas, kills me and does not wish to help me!

Oh miserable, ignominious fate,
That the only person in the whole wide world who can give me life,
Alas, gives me naught but death!

Yvette recalled having sung the first soprano part of this particular madrigal at
the Pimpleton Heights Prep Academy with its Collegium Musicum, just prior to
the pandemic, and also remembered having read that its composer, Carlo Gesualdo,
who was the Prince of Venosa and Count of Conza had—by some historical accounts, in a fit of passionate rage, and by other more modern (and allegedly reliable)
accounts, in a premeditated fashion, with the aid of four armed men on the night of
16 October, 1590—murdered his wife, Princess Maria D'Avalos, by stabbing her re-
peatedly with his sword when he had caught her in bed with her lover, the Duke of
Andria. In some accounts it is indicated that Gesualdo himself had murdered both
his wife and her lover, and in other more modern accounts that he had murdered
his wife and left the work of murdering her lover to his four armed accomplices.
In any case, all accounts indicate it was a brutal and bloody carnifice that left both
corpses in grotesque, mutilated condition. Hearing and watching the dark moody
madrigal performed by this elegant consort of voices gave our heroine dire fore-
bodings as to what belikely lay in store for her. She prayed to her Lord and Savior
that the madrigal wasn't a portent of things to come.

Whilst being modeled around the market by the quintet of stern authoritative
black-suited men, Yvette was momentaneously mesmerized not only by the strains
of the madrigal itself, which she already knew by rote, but also by the ultra polished
rendition thereof by this captivating consort of singers, barely noticing that as she
was being paraded through the aisles she was also being pinched, goosed, spanked,
creamed, combed, kissed, rubbed, scrubbed, fondled, groped, and sucked upon by
mostly random strangers but also by a few people she vaguely recognized from her
college classes, including one of the school's adjunct professors who taught a section
she attended twice a week for her class in Feline Transgender Studies. In the course
of carrying her cross and dragging her chains through her martyrdom, Yvette could
not help but observe that Mildred's Market had undergone recently a major-league
high-tech upgrade, including the installation of what appeared to be some kind of
weird conveyor belt like thingumajig she had never laid her eyes upon before.

The quintet of black-suited stern authoritative men escorted Yvette to what
appeared to be a medical station of sorts that had been set up in front of the delicatessen, next to one of the checkout counters that had a gleaming gold-plated cash
register upon it. A tall handsome gentleman in a white knee-length overcoat, who
appeared to be a high-ranking medical professional, was prepping a grotesquely
ginormous hypodermic syringe barrel with an unusually long and boogery looking

pair of needles. The man was pointing the needles upwards and gently tapping the barrel of the syringe with his right forefinger to move its air bubbles to the top.

"Ah, excellent!" said the doctor upon laying his eyes on Yvette. "You can unleash her now and remove her cuffs. The Felicity Conveyor is sufficiently versatile to handle things if she gets too twitchy or jumpy whilst I administer her injection."

Now that the madrigal had concluded and was followed by the pick-up quintet of principal string players from the symphony and the Italian vocal consort collaborating together in a rendition of a chamber arrangement of the Lacrimosa movement from Mozart's Requiem, Yvette felt a sudden surge of panic, as she had no idea what these people were planning to do with her. The black-suited quintet of stern authoritative men flipped her over so that she was lying face down upon the stainless steel belt of this so-called "Felicity Conveyor" in front of a gathering audience. Some computerized leather-covered metal slats on the conveyor belt automatically elevated her ultimatum and spread out her cheeks so that the raspberry-like hole of her inner sanctum was made visible for public scrutiny.

'Twas approximately 2:00 PM on a cold blustery Thursday afternoon in late November. Normally, Mildred's Market had an excellent climate-controlled system that maintained a temperature of between 68 and 72 degrees Fahrenheit, regardless of how inclement the weather was outdoors, but today, for some odd and unknown reason, the windows of the store were wide open, not only giving outsiders an opportunity to peer inside the store so they could take in the spectacle of Yvette's public shaming but also, apparently, to enhance her physical discomfort into the bargain, as she could feel the stiff breeze blowing into the most sun-deprived nooks of her anatomy, making her feel even more self-conscious at being as naked as a worm in a crowded public environment.

A tall imperious looking gentleman with a powerful and commanding presence approached her directly from an office behind the deli. He stared directly into her eyes as he stepped towards her and she immediately recognized him as the owner and manager of Mildred's Market, Eiden's presumptive father: Herr Justyce Dreadmiller. Quite naturally, she could envision a host of other by far preferable scenarios in which to be formally introduced to the man she had hoped would become her father-in-law in the not too distant future. It caused her to blush into what she imagined must have been the deepest shade of crimson ever witnessed in the history of humankind. She had never before felt so mortified in all her life! It was even worse than having her temperature taken rectally in front of four hostile witnesses in the relative comfort and privacy of her apartment, as had transpired not an hour before.

Mr. Dreadmiller glared into her orbits with a deep glowering grimace of violent revulsion, as if someone had just taken a dump on his dinner plate, whereupon he broke asudden into an uncontrollable fit of maniacal laughter, almost to the point where he was literally rolling on the floor. His laughter was so infectious, in fact, that it spread in waves throughout the audience assembled inside and outside the market. These outbursts of cachinnations and hysterics occurred in violent juxta-position to the somber strains of the Lacrimosa movement of Mozart's Requiem as it was being performed with the strictest of all sobriety and the gravest of all solemnity by singers and instrumentalists of the very highest caliber.

As soon as the "Amen!" of the Lacrimosa concluded, Mr. Dreadmiller cleared his throat before speaking through a set of microphones belonging to an ultra fancy high-tech public address system that amplified his voice throughout the store and out onto the streets for at least a decade of city blocks on all sides. "I'm so pleased you were able to make it to our inauguration ceremony this afternoon, Mademoiselle Cartier," he said in a gracious, almost deferential, tone, the very model of gentility and civility. His manner of speaking reminded Yvette of his son Eiden, who was a smooth talker in his own right. "As I have no doubt you already have a fair idea as to what the underlying grounds are for your being summoned here to participate in today's celebration, I needn't bore you—or your audience, for that matter—with the formality of offering you any kind of detailed explanation apropos of the whys and wherefores of your attendance here this afternoon. And, if you don't quite get the drift thereof at this stage of the game, I personally guarantee that you shall in short order."

Yvette's nude body quivered involuntarily not just from the chill of the gusts of wind blowing in from outdoors but even more so from the discomfiting collywobbles induced within her by the ominous undertone of Mr. Dreadmiller's so-called welcome speech, to say nothing of the enormous size of the hypodermic needles and syringe barrel that were being flourished by a certifiable looking medical specialist, accoutered in a crumpled white lab coat, who was proudly stationed upon an elevated rotating turntable in the center aisle of the market. Our poor subdebutante had somehow or other mistakenly assumed earlier on that, in the wake of having been spanked so relentlessly upon her exposed posterior by President Ulrich Armstrong in the presence of three individuals who had made no bones about razzing and scoffling her in order to compound the kankerdort of her downcoming, that she had already borne her cross and that, upon being enlight-ened as to the crooked and devious avenues of her ignominious ways, her trials and tribulations had thenabouts been adjudged concluded and that her long-term penance thereafterward would merely consist of her being mandated to attend a community college for the purpose of proving herself to be a competent, if not slightly above average, student, whereupon she would thenceforward walk a righ-teous path to her deliverance from her past sins and their resultant consequences. It was only now slowly beginning to dawn upon her, however, that the spankings and scoldings she had just abrooked so bravely at the hands of Professor Armstrong and her ex-boss Celine, within the confines of her luxurious living accommodations, constituted an aperitif to the multi-course banquet of correctional regimens that was evidently scheduled, in accordance with some *menu à prix fixe*, to be inflicted upon her exposed flesh, judging from the general tenor of the milieu wherewithin she currently found herself so defenselessly ensconced.

"Before we commence our official celebration of the 25th anniversary of the grand opening of Mildred's Market, as well as the formal inauguration of this ingenious Japanese-manufactured, award-winning appliance, known in American non-vernacular English as an "At-Your-Beck Felicity Conveyor," I wish to personally express to you, Mademoiselle Cartier, my sincere and unbounded gratitude for the astonishing success we have thus far had with our special fundraising efforts. We have already more than quadrupled our initial pledge of $90,000.00, having at this point raised upwards of $400,000.00—*and counting!* I want you to know that the television commercials that featured highlights from your masturbation marathons contributed substantially to our success in advertising this event."

Mr. Dreadmiller gave the hot red stripes on Yvette's oiled behind an almost affectionate rub, which quickened her pulse some and caused a mild stirring sensation inside her. She darted nervous glances around the store and noticed, for the first time, several giant telescreens mounted on mobile adjustable robotic arms, dangling from the ceiling and also from small multi-rotor drones that were flying around the boutique, that featured continuous video footage of her Spoilt Highness strapped unclothed to the crocodile leather futon in her apartment with Eiden oiling and spanking her bare bum cheeks with an expression of amused derision, interspersed with ticks of triumphant glee, on his gloriously handsome phizog, which was twisted into a satisfied smirk as he intermittently turned his head around to wink and give a thumb's-up to the camera that had apparently been surveilling all of her activities in her apartment unbeknownst to her. This scene and others that followed were interspersed with short clips of her shoplifting sprees in the pharmaceutical section of Mildred's Market. When the spanking scene eventually faded out, some newfangled ultra high-resolution footage of our heroine playing with herself in the shower faded in, zooming out from a low-angle view of her clean-shaven vulva being vigorously frigged by her using a penetrative sex toy, interspersed with shoulder-level footage of her exquisite countenance in varying states of near hyperventilation, which lasted two or three minutes until she reached her "Big O," whereupon the most embarrassing imaginable footage of her lewd activities faded in immediately thereafter (in sync with the shower scene fading out), which featured close-up footage (with the volume control turned up to its maximum level) of our heroine in the altogether maniacally sucking upon giant silicone penises whilst impaling herself on vibrating dildos of varying shapes and sizes and, in the worst of all possible worst-case scenarios, calling out, atwixt her impassioned moans and groans, the name of none other than Professor Ulrich Armstrong (on whom she'd long harbored a secret schoolgirl crush) begging him, in the height of her phrenzied masturbatorial ecstasies, to spank and punish her without mercy for being such a bad, naughty, horny little cumguzzler, on her bare-naked seat-of-vengeance, and to bone her like a stray dog up her tight little bunghole—hard, long, and fast. It was

embarrassing beyond belief to have thousands of spectators not only casually viewing this consummately professional film footage (with ultra high production values)
of her astonishing variety of masturbatorial bodily contortions but, even worse
than that, to have them hearken so engrossedly to her most obscenely salacious
sexual fantasies as they were being so fiercely, forcefully, and incisively vociferated
by her mellifuous coloratura voice via the multiple channels of an ultra high quality
speaker system positioned strategically throughout Mildred's Market and out onto
the neighboring arterials for upwards of a mile and a half everywhither, even
extending beyond the outermost purlieus of the central business district into the
adjoining residential communities of this tight-knit little suburban municipality,
where everyone and their uncle-in-laws seemed to know one another like the back
of a book.

Because she harbored similar eroto-romantic crushes on many other professors
whose classes she'd attended over the years, not only at Pimpleton State but also at
the Pimpleton Heights Prep Academy, she now found herself fretting her soul in
mortal fear and trepidation that the tigress had been let out of the bag, so to speak,
and that it would now only be a matter of the fleetingest interval of time before she
would find herself laureled as not only the japing- but also the spanking-stick of the
community, and that, furtherover, the she-she talk and tattle-boxing by quidnuncs
and blabbermouths would be relayed all over the map on latrine wirelesses, not
just inwith the vicinage of the Pimpleton retropolitan area but also far beyond its
exurban boundaries. The fact that her most perverted algophilic fantasies and sado-
masochistic pack-rape rampings were out for the world to leer at, feast upon, and
letch over was, from her subjective perverspective, way beyond the bounds of being
unbideable, for it denuded her of every lingering vestige of her elsewise inscrutable
girly-girl mystique, an anomalous feminine phenomenon by which she set great
store, acknowledging it as a precious gift from her creator. All these professors,
whose names she had babbled out loud whilst frigging herself vigorously in what
she had initially presumed to be unsurveilled settings, would be promptly apprised
of prezactly what she yearned for each and every one of them to do to all the private
nooks and crannies of her unshielded flesh, which was, in essence, tantamount to a
carte blanche for them to take whatever liberties they liked, unencumbered by the
bureaucrappic inconveniences of begging her permission to do so, as they would
all know by the end of the hour that she would simply melt in their arms and
even go the extra mile to plead with them to drill and discipline her in whatsoever ways they saw fit, irregardless of the lengths to which she would go to feign
disinterest in being abused thuswise for their sovereign pleasure. The wholesale
declassification of this personal intelligence on her nymphomaniacal appetites and
other sexual perversions was so insufferably disconcerting, not to say unspeakably
dehumiligradiing, for our Spoilt Highness, that she felt allutterly beside herself with
ferblitzed discumfuddlement! It was bad enough that she never wanted anyone in
the whole wide world to know anything about her secret sexual infatuation for the

dean & president of Pimpleton State, but even worse if members of the community as a whole were to ascertain how compulsively promiscuous she was in the vast preponderance of her private sexual fantasies as regards hundreds, if not thousands, of other stern, authoritative, middle-aged alpha-male figures she had encountered over the years in the close & tight-knit community of Pimpleton Heights (not discluding her envisioned future father-in-law, Herr Dreadmiller). Although she tended to be unconquerably shy and reserved in her overall bearing, she was on the flip side extraordinarily effusive insofar as expressing her most deliriously savage and unhingedly perverted sexual fantasies apropos of specific authoritative male individuals in the community, calling out their names loud and clear whensoever she buttered her muffin or glazed her doughnut in what she had assumed in all innocence to be an unsurveilled private setting behind tightly secured deadbolted doors.

Looking around the store she noticed, for the first time, dozens of exquisitely printed, full-color, glossy 22 by 34-inch flyers mounted on the walls throughout the space (and, presumably, all over town) advertising the inauguration celebration of the designated "At-Your-Beck Felicity Conveyor," whose belted roller bed she had just been physically deposited upon. What bothered her most about these flyers was that they featured high-resolution nude photographic images of her in some incredibly compromising positions that were evidently taken during her long-drawn-out day-and-night masturbation marathons when she had all the while been under the erroneous assumption that she had been alone and unseen in the cherished privacy of her spanking new digs (no pun intended). Each poster was a one-of-a-kind edition unto itself featuring uniquely exclusive sexually explicit photographs of Yvette Cartier with comic-book-style dialogue balloons connected to her nabble-trap with the names and honorifics, in big bold bright red fluorescent fonts followed by over-emphatic triple exclamation points, of one or more professors from Pimpleton State Luniversity and/or the Pimpleton Heights Prep Academy printed inside them (to say nothing of other stern authoritative middle-aged alpha males from the community, such as the police chief, the town mayor, and several dozen court-appointed judges). Each poster was accompanied by a small pair of digital headphones and digital control panels connected to the walls that enabled any meddlers, curiosity seekers, and/or info-holics off the street to listen to short uncensored clips highlighting our subdebutante's passionately vociferated masturbatorial visions during the ecstatic culminations of her points of no return (that is to say, whenever she was on the brink of reaching an irreversible momentum towards the glorious consummation of her crowning summits of amorous effervescences), and, more specifically, when she called out their names and begged them, in explicitly enunciated detail (howsoever sordidly fescennine such solicitations for her ultimate masturbatisfaction might be), as to what prezactly she itched for them to do to her defenseless young figure whilst sprawled out in abject submission to their every wayward whim & fancy.

"Ah, yes," continued Justyce Dreadmiller with his impassioned monopologue, addressing Mademoiselle Cartier directly, with a shrewd expression on his mug, as though he could read her like a book. "I can discern a spark of crystal clarity in thine eyes, my sweet, notwithstanding all the penitential tear-blobs that are beyond question occluding thy vision at this revelatory light-bulb of a moment. We have Eiden's fiancée Francine Armstrong—who happens to be my son's friend Werther's first cousin, and who is best known as my good friend Ulrich's eldest daughter— to thank for her brilliant technical work setting up the hidden cameras and audio/ visual surveillance equipment inside your apartment."

Wait, what...? thought Yvette. Had she just heard that right? Eiden's *fiancée...?*

"The fact that you never even noticed you were being surveilled," continued Mr. Dreadmiller, "is testament to Ms. Armstrong's consummate professionalism. It should come as no great surprise to you, then, when I share with you that Francine happens to be one of the most sought-after surveillance engineers in the country, if not the entire planet. In fact, she's not only an impressively accomplished young woman in that particular field but in a host of others as well. I can personally avouch, for example (having heard her perform Elliott Carter's Night Fantasies with panache and aplomb), that she is an outstanding concert pianist, specializing in all periods and styles of classical music, including some famously challenging twentieth- and twenty-first-century works by the likes of composers Brian Ferneyhough, Kaikhosru Shapurji Sorabji, Gary Lloyd Noland, György Ligeti, Joseph Fennimore, and Frederic Rzewski, among others. She's also a skilled multi-linguist, fluent in French, German, Italian, Spanish, Portuguese, Russian, Japanese, Greek, Latin, and Hebrew; Egyptian & Levantine Arabic; Mandarin, Wu & Yue Chinese; and boasts a thorough and comprehensive reading knowledge of at least two dozen other languages, including Sanskrit, Aramaic, and Old Norse. She is reputed, in high circles, to possess the rare talent of being able to master a language unfamiliar to her in less than a week, and in some cases over the course of a mere weekend. Morefurther, she's an author of several peer-reviewed books on arcane scientific topics (which are way above my head) that are currently used as textbooks in many graduate level courses worldwide. At age eighteen, Francine Armstrong had been, for the fourth year in a row, considered as an eligible candidate for a Nobel Prize in Physics, so it's most probably only a matter of time (perhaps a year or two) before the esteemed members of the Norwegian Nobel Committee buckle down and finally select her for the prize she most richly deserves, to wit: the most coveted prize in the world, 'the prize to end all prizes,' as it's been fitly yclept. On top of all that, she's a long-distance marathon runner, having won first place in several such events in the past four or five years, as well as a silver-medalist Olympic swimmer. What also impresses me about Francine Armstrong is that, aside from being a fabulous cook, she has never failed to find time to spend with her loved ones and has always proven herself serviceable, above and beyond the call of duty, at taking care of her younger siblings whensoever the need has presented itself. As you can well imagine, I have nothing but the highest admiration and respect for this young lady, whom I proudly look forward to calling my daughter-in-law in the near future, for I am ever so pleased to officially announce this after that Francine and my son Eiden have formally announced their engagement and are scheduled to walk down the aisle on the sixth of next month!"

As Yvette burst into tears on hearing tell of Mr. Dreadmiller's definitive confirmation that she had just been jilted by the love of her life, these tidings were met by a spontaneous outburst of thunderous applause from the audience, which at this point in time consisted of hundreds, if not thousands, of Bacchanalians, merrymakers, and carousers who were gathered inside the store and out on all the adjoining streets. Most of downtown Pimpleton Heights had been cordoned off by law enforcement officials rigged out in riot gear, with military backup having been furnished by the National Guard, who were standing at the ready, lest anything untoward occur.

Mr. Dreadmiller shifted his attention towards Yvette once again. "Now," he cautioned her with an almost paternal solicitude, "breathe in deeply, my child, and prepare for your injection." Upon seeing teardrops flowing silently down her crestfallen countenance, he added, "Of course, I would be lying to you if I told you it won't hurt. It most assuredly *will* hurt, for the experience of pain is part and parcel of being disciplined for your transgressions and malefactions."

Terrified at the sight of the mastodonic hypodermic syringe barrel, with a pair of sharp disposable needles attached to it that looked to be over two feet in length, being vambrashed by a quintet of half-crazed looking medical professionals in crumpled lab coats, our agitable subdebutante took a poke at screaming at the top of her lungs. The computerized sensors of the Felicity Conveyor, however, beat her to the punch by immediately locking her mouth with a silicone ball gag. When she struggled to regain her upright posture and make a run for it, the sensors of the Felicity Conveyor did their job once again by strapping her securely face-down in leather-padded metal wrist & ankle restraints from which it was impossible to break loose. Three of the five lab-coated medical professionals approached her, one teasingly wigwagging the hypodermic needles and syringe barrel in front of her face whilst the other two swabbed her exposed nether cheeks with a scented disinfectant solution using a pair of massive cotton-tipped applicators. The swabbing went on for upwards of five to ten minutes and had the effect of cooling her posterior to such a degree—compounded by the stiff breeze blowing in from outdoors—that she became all the more conscious of how unambiguously bare-assed she was in front of hundreds, if not thousands, of total strangers, all of whom were dressed to the teeth in high winter gear. During this ritual, the assemblage of onlookers, as well as several dozen video camera operators from various local, national, and international news networks, had gathered within spanking reach of our helpless young victim to watch in awe-struck silence as they shot exclusive footage of her thrutched features and quivering differential during the dramatic countdown to her dorsogluteal hypodermic injections into both cheeks of her flaming catastrophe. Yvette did everything in her power to control herself from detonating with a savage, almost murtherous orgasm.

"No need to be alarmed, my child," said Mr. Dreadmiller, "Permit me to introduce you to five of my nearest and dearest old buddies, all of whom are long-standing members of the Pimpleton Heights City Council: Herr Doktors Lobotticelli, Ampukoviç, Sawitov, Needlebutt, und Sphincteramus. They will be injecting your bumper with an aphrodisiacal medicament called Lubricitrophin, which was just approved this morning by the FDA. After the pain on your injection site fades, which will take only three or four minutes, and this powerful solution circulates through your bloodstream, you will start feeling your pulse quickening, your blood pumping, and your face flushing as your perspiration glands go into high gear in conjunction with experiencing delicious muscle convulsions in your anus, vagina, and uterus. What Lubricitrophin achieves, with minimal side effects, is the prolongation of these pre-orgasmic bodily reactions to being sexually aroused, which will delay your reaching the ultimate resolution phase of your climax but will instead vacillate back and forth between the excitement and plateau phases thereof for hours on end, and once the resolution phase of your sexual climax *is* achieved, this process will repeat itself over and over again for upwards of a fortnight (give or take), albeit with diminishing returns as the intensity in effect of the medicament gradually subsides. As the oscillations between phases of your sexual climax decrease, however, the frequency of orgasms will increase almost exponentially for a period of nine to twelve days.

"Once I had come to the sobering realization that your filchings of my merchandise over the past two and a half years had added up to losses of inventory amounting to upwards of $90,000.00 in wholesale revenues and $150,000.00 in projected retail revenues, it became the breaking threshold for me in terms of what I was willing and able to tolerate in financial losses, as I had planned on doing some necessary and important renovations and technical upgrades to my business. As you will soon discover on your own, the At-Your-Beck Felicity Conveyor is an ingeniously constructed apparatus, something that only the Japanese, with their meticulous attention to minute details (and not even the Germans or Swiss), are capable of inventing and developing. The time is now upon us, without further ado, to commence the inaugural celebration of the unveiling of this fine new piece of machinery!"

Our disconcerted subdebutante felt the pair of hypodermic needles, which were undoubtedly sharp enough to split the hair on a fairyfly's antennae, pierce through her skin and plunge subcutaneously deep into the right & left cheeks of her arse. She wanted to scream from the pain but the ball gag wouldn't permit her to do so, nor was there any way for her to dodge the plunging needles, as the AI-prompted restraints held her arms, legs, and lends securely in place. All she could do at this moment was submit to her trial by ordeal without complaint or movement, her only solace from suffering being her appearingly bottomless well of penitential teardrops, as the crowd of eagerly inquisitive spectators watched in nighwhat cat-apleptic enthrallment as she afforced futilitously to struggle out of her obstructing restraints and scree-out for mercy.

As promised by Mr. Dreadmiller, the pain was well-nigh intolerable, enough so to momentanely distract our heroine from the sheer humiliation of her mis-adventure. Once the pain had subsided some, she observed the ever energetic and resourceful Celine manning one of the cash registers in the delicatessen that had a large crowd of individuals waiting in line to purchase various sex toys from her warehouse and almost immediately thereafter opening the containers in which they were wrapped to apply sex lubricants to whatever playthings and novelties they had just bought, which included dildos in all forms, shapes and sizes, anal vibrators, butt plugs, dog leashes, nipple tweezers, magic bean clips, stainless steel adjustable pussy clamps, and a host of other personal pleasure objects. What alarmed Yvette even more was that a number of the customers, many of whom were sipping martinis and partaking of what looked to be incredibly delicious hors d'oeuvres, were also copping punishment paddles of manifold sizes and thicknesses with holes in them. She had read that the holes in such implements were known to maximize the pain when one was spanked with them due to a much lower degree of air cushioning when swung robustly at their targets, which some victims have been known to liken to the sensation of being stung by a swarm of angry-as-hell hornets bent on exacting a torrent of severe retributions (for God only knows what reason) upon their targeted prey.

The computerized robotic sensors in the Felicity Conveyor loosened Yvette's restraints so that she could move more freely once again. This time she manifested a marked reluctance to make any further attempts at escaping (which, commend-ably, was a rapid-fire Pavlovian response to her having been professionally con-ditioned into a state of meek yet sullen submission), especially as there was no viable window of opportunity to do so, nor any place she knew of where she could run and hide from her tormentors. The quintet of black-suited stern authoritative men approached her from all sides and hoisted her up into a seated position, lifting and securing her heels into metal stirrups. One of them was wearing a pair of powered exoskeleton latex gloves and, without warning, started to apply mentho-lated lubricants inside her mystery zone and front passage whilst the others without gloves on applied lubricants vigorously over each and every other inch of her flesh, including her nipples, which immediately hardened upon touch when palpated. Al-ready, she noticed that the overall effect of the Lubricitrophin was to intensify, and otherwise aggravate, the nagging little itch in her belly to the point where it felt as though she was on the cusp of achieving her ultimate thrill, albeit devoid of the power to effectively arrive at her cherished destination. It made her surrealize, then and there, that there was a fine line of distinction to be drawn between the sen-sation of blushing a deep hue of crimson (as she nodoubtedly was at this moment from the overwhelming shame of being sexually humiliated in front of thousands of drooling spectators who were licking their chops in anticipation of some pre-scripted denouement) and that of achieving her ultimate pleasure. As she was being vigorously rubbed down by these hard men, she caught sight of her lover, Eiden, standing arm in arm with his beautiful young fiancée Francine Armstrong, both of whom appeared, from the looks of loving affection in their eyes, to be complacently contented with each other. They glanced at our succourless ingénude obliquely with transparent looks of blissful Schadenfreude on their cruel physiognomies. Yvette couldn't tell what hurt more, the pain of being publicly diminuated to the town mocking-stock or the pain of being romantically abjectated by the man of her dreams and love of her life.

The fact that the surveillance engineer Francine was a first cousin of Werther's somehow caused our debased subdebutante to feel even greener with jealousy than if Eiden's fiancée had not in fact been connected with her ex-beau's boon compan-ion by blood, as if, in some strange and inexplicable way, Werther Nemesinovich had managed to serve our heroine his own unique recipe of punitive comeuppances on an ice-cold platter in recompense for the crucifying afflictions that had long been known to wreak havoc on his heart and soul by the simple empirical fact of her having cocked up her neb to his gallantizing suitorings, as was very likely the case, presumably, in respect to all the other nameless souls she had taken advantage of over the years. It was hard for her to think things out with any semblance of lucidity or brightness of insight whilst being so vigorously lubricated with amorous oils from tit to toe and, furtherover, feeling the stiff salty breeze from the ocean caressing the most intimate parts of her anatomy. As soon as the quintet of lubri-cators had completed their anatomical task, a loud bell sounded, whereupon Justyce Dreadmiller stepped forth to the podium, as if on cue, in front of the microphones dangling from the boom arms of the public address system.

CHAPTER FOURTEEN

"And now, Dandies and Gentledames," announced the neighborhood grocer, "the Inauguration of our 'At-Your-Beck Felicity Conveyor' shall commence!" This was followed by cheers and applause from the grocery boutique's employees and patrons, as well as the thousand-and-one merrymakers and carousers drinking and dancing on the streets outside the market.

Yvette noticed that scores of people had stationed themselves at various points in the store through which the belt conveyor was slated to make its run and were wielding in their hands what appeared to be the sex toys and discipline tools they had just purchased from Celine when she had manned the gold-plated till just a few short minutes agone.

Yvette could not help but assume that Mildred's Market must have been making an unprecedented killing from this fundraiser, especially judging from the lavish spread of cocktails, hors d'oeuvres, and vintage wines she saw laid out for the fundraiser's attendees. On one table she could make out large plates of deviled eggs, stuffed mushrooms, and pickled shrimp; on another table were gilded platters of Medina dates from Saudi Arabia stuffed with artisan sausages and what she guessed were most probably chunks of Boar's Head Chèvre goat cheese. Another platter on the same table was laid out with crispy fritters that looked like spinach bhajias made with grated (presumably organic) carrots, onions, and ginger, accompanied by small bowls of home-made mango chutney, adjacent to which was another enormous platter housing bowls of what appeared to be bourbon chicken liver paté served with cornichons and rosemary crackers, vanilla butter anchovy toasts, Brussel sprouts with bacon jam impaled upon gleaming brass pins, silver beaded spears, golden snakes and other decorative toothpicks. She saw one fat patron gorging himself on cheesy samosa puffs that he kept dipping into bowls of green chutney and ketchup, another even fatter patron who was stuffing himself with toasted European white truffle ravioli dipped in marinara sauce, and another morbidly obese patron packing away dozens of miniature mirabelle marzipan tarts and showing very little consideration for the young ones behind him who wanted to partake of their own share of these selfsame goodies. To her immediate right she saw a cute pair of twin girls in Mary-Jane dresses gorging on smoked trout croquettes, and on her immediate left she saw a thin, funereal Kafkaesque gentleman sipping a "Diamond is Forever" Martini, with a one-carat diamond at the bottom of his glass, in the company of a silver-haired, dowdily dressed old woman wearing coke-bottle barnacles (his wife peradventure) who aligned with the common prototype of an elementary school librarian, sipping on a twelve-thousand-dollar Ono Champagne Cocktail.

The bell pealed loudly once again, almost deafening our abashed young demi-vierge, whereupon the low hum of an electric motor started sounding, causing a faint vibration to buzz beneath her groin, quite possibly for the purpose of stimulating her vagina. From what she could glean from her observations, it appeared that she was at the head of the Felicity Conveyor, which, in itself, upon close inspection, bore little if any resemblance to a conventional belt conveyor, as far as she could discern, but rather appeared to be comprised of a pastiche of belt-conveying mechanisms all working in tandem under the authoritarian intelligence of a masterminding control network that was guided, to a large extent (she assumed), by AI. It looked like a glorious feat of engineering technology, as she observed, on the one hand, loops of flexible rubberlike material that were being stretched between rollers controlled by three-phase squirrel-cage induction motors that had just been activated, interspersed with the employment of chains, spirals, hydraulics, and other gears, gadgets, and mechanisms (including rotary-jointed articulated manipulators, Cartesian manipulators with vacuum cup hands, and dual-function ladle grippers for scooping up liquids, among other things) to process and move cargo off and on the belt. As our subdebutante possessed very little by way of engineering know-how (she was about as clueless as an unborn fetus in that regard), she had considerable difficulty ascribing what the intended functions of these divers and sundry electro-robotic contrivances (that were clicking, rattling, and chirping about her from every which way) were.

The conveyor belt commenced transporting Ms. Cartier slowly through various sections of the store, beginning in the general vicinity of the delicatessen. As long as she didn't fidget too much or make any abrupt movements or gestures that would send red flags to the machine that she was planning on breaking loose and making a run for it, the AI hardware in the Felicity Conveyor allowed her to shift from one side to another and move about quite freely and effortlessly on the belt as she was being transported through the shop. If she overstepped her bounds by as much as a micrometer (give or take), a medium voltage electrical shock would be administered upon her uncovered kaboolies and labonza as a courteous reminder to keep herself in line. A Utopia pillow emerged through an opening in the belt so that she could lean back comfortably and rest her head thereupon in the event that she felt any inward inclination to luxuriate in her tormentuous travails.

The first in an extended series of correctional measures drawing a bead upon Yvette's privy parts (which caught our poor girl completely off guard) was a consecution of stone-cold jets of a creamy spooge-like substance that was being shot by Celine and others from a battery of high-end premium electric manually operated faux-sperm guns attached to the Felicity Conveyor on both sides (which, not unlike the handheld squirt guns employed earlier by her adversaries, also had long-range high pressure capacities). The spooge-like gloop was so glacially frigid upon impact that it stung Yvette's bare belly and back-parts with a vengeance. After being shot for a minute or two with this amorphous gooey substance a series of small lateral whisks and beaters dispersed the viscous fluid all over our wayward ingénude's exposed flesh, which felt like someone was playing a game of creep-mouse on her from tit to toe, causing her at times to cackle unwittingly. In the next few minutes, before the Felicity Conveyor transported our discomposed subdebutante into an enclosed section of the machine belonging to the dairy department, she felt herself being deep-fingered inside her pussyhole, pinched acutely on her midriff and mammaries, and goosed aggressively betwixt her bum cheeks from every quarter by random hotheads who were restlessly awaiting their turns in line to cop gratuitous feels of our groveled young coed's curvacious anatomy. Some people were evidently there merely for the thrill of taking in such a sight for sore eyes, whilst others were there to exact condign retributions upon the principal object of their grievances. The atmosphere was chaotic, reminding our coquette of hundreds of harried airline passengers bearishly butting in front of one another, like the Grobians one typically sees at baggage reclaim carousels to repossess their luggage in packed retropolitan air transportation terminals. Amidst the pandemonium she caught occasional glimpses of familiar faces, including those of some famous fashionistas she admired, not to mention mobs of randy drool- and muscle-boys from her prep & college classes whom she had prickteased without mercy (and not without Phallus aforethought) yet never even given the steam off her piss to please, as they say. As soon as she was deposited "safely" inside the enclosed compartment of the dairy chamber, the Felicity Conveyor ground to an abrupt halt, at which instant it flipped her automatically onto her backside, like a hot-holding street dog being tonged by a vendor from a pan of near boiling water into a bun, and lifted her into a semi-seated position atop of a vibrating sex saddle, as in a recliner, attaching the nipples on her breasts to soft rubber liners with suction hoses on them that appeared to be aspiring to function as milkers. These supposed milkers had hard stainless steel exteriors and were attached to a milking machine of sorts, though Yvette had guessed correctly that its purpose was not to milk her breasts per se but rather to harden the nipples thereupon so as to aggravate her sexual euphoria and paranoia, thus: "paraphoria." After the suction hoses had done their job, Yvette was flipped back over onto her belly and gently sodomized with a robotic vibrating butt plug with a mug shot of Donald J. Trump engraved upon it that was attached to wiring that ran along the conveyor belt. When the machine spat her out into public view once again, she heard spontaneous outbursts of hysterical laughter from all sides, knowing that the vibrating butt plug was very likely the source of their mirth. Being on the verge of reaching a state of indescribable ecstasy, yet also being physiologically blocked by the Lubricitrophin from doing so at the same time, greatly intensified her feelings of—what was it?—sexual awkwardness. She couldn't even begin to describe it, nor did she yet know for certain whether she hated it with all her might or loved it with all her heart.

As if out of left field, her governess Prunelda appeared in a panel that opened directly above her, at which point the Felicity Conveyor ground to a screeching halt once again, as if sensing through the agency of its artificial intelligence that Prunelda wished to have a special word with her young charge. Before Yvette could get a handle on the situation, a lubed silicone-tipped shaft from a high-speed thrusting drilldo sex machine that was connected to the Felicity Conveyor began penetrating her love hole as if it knew in advance where all her pleasure spots were located, which only served to compound the awkwardness of her embarrassment at being beheld in this fashion (and worse, from only inches away) by her superannuated, prissy old governess.

"Tsk, tsk, tsk!" chided Prunelda in that charmless neo-Victorian voice of hers. "Just look at thyself, Yvette! Just look at thyself, *wontcha?* How does it make you feel...? Prithee tell me, dear child: What, in the name of all that is holy, do you imagine you're going to tell your grandchildren one day, by way of explanation, when they catch the videographic footage of your disgraceful exhibitionistic behavior on Saturday morning TV some thirty years hence? Just what in God's name are you going to tell them...?"

"Yeah!" shouted a thousand and one voices in unison from throughout the aisles of the store and from tens of blocks outside it. "What are you going to tell them...?" Yvette was rudely stunned upon taking forth that Prunelda's voice had been amplified throughout the purlieus of the central business district and, most probably, its environing suburbs.

Our overwrought young coquette was so bitterly ashamed at being seen and confronted in this fashion by her stern and unforgiving governess (let alone by thousands of random strangers on the streets) with nary a hole in the ground she knew of into which she could duck her pretty young head to hide her flushed countenance, not just from her governess Prunelda but from all the others as well, that she broke out into a disconsolate fit of the most abject imaginable contrition. It was only at this point in time that Yvette had come to the conscious sur-realization that Prunelda had taken charge of a remote-control monitor attached to the Felicity Conveyor that determined the strength of the thrusts of the Drilldo that had seemingly taken its own initiative insofar as callously rummaging through her dearest bodily part. The Lubricitrophin had kicked in to such an astonishingly intense degree that an extraordinarily high plateau of pre-climactic suspense could now be maintained devoid of any imminent danger in the immediate future of a humiliating resolution thereto going down just yet (not to say that the prolonged procrasturbatory irresolution of her carnal cravings was any less degrading from our subdebutante's perverspective).

"You've brought naught but shame and disgrace upon your loving guardians, Evie!" chided Prunelda severely. "I can't even begin to tell you how disappointed they are at the revelations of your academic dishonesty—especially seeing as they are such highly respected scholars themselves in their own specialized areas of expertise. If only you had stuck with Werther Nemesinovich, who seems like such a nice young man, instead of leading him on like you did and then running off with those expensive diamond earrings from Tiffany's, which cost the poor fellow more than an entire summer's earnings from his miserable day job at the sewage treatment plant, then none of what we are witnessing here today would ever have transpired, as I'm wholly confident that Werther would have kept you on a tight leash to curb you from your congenitally profligate ways.

"I think it only fair, by the bye, that you should now be informed that your guardians have tossed all your belongings out onto the curb in front of their house, and I can already attest unequivocally to the fact that scores of vagrants, junkies, and gang members are helping themselves to your most prized worldly possessions, including your collection of Gucci handbags, Prada miniskirts, jewelry from Tiffany's (including those beautiful earrings Werther gave you), and a host of other personal effects, not the least of which are those disgustingly offensive handwritten diaries of yours that you were hiding under your mattress. A good number of the local, national, and even international news networks (quite notably the BBC, CNN, Fox News, CBC, Al Jazeera, and many others) are already quoting excerpts from those appalling journals, and the widespread opinion polls which have thus far been conducted all over the planet (not discluding remote archipelagos such as the Tristan da Cunha in the South Atlantic, Eastern Island in the South Pacific, the Changtang region on the Tibetan Plateau, the extreme highland communities of the Peruvian Andes, the South Pole Station in Antarctica, and Siberian towns near the North Pole, to name just a few) are unanimous, on both the extreme left and right of the political spectrum, in their vehement condemnation of the sum & substance of your unconscionable scribblings. The broad consensus gleaned from these international opinion polls is that your private journals are beyond the pale. Not only are they shocking and shameful insofar as what they reflect of the flawed moral character of their diarist, but each and every page is virtually swarming with libelous insinuations about those nearest and dearest to said scribbler. Your guardians will never forgive you for some of the things you've written about them. Nor will *I*, young wench, for what you've written about *me*. A 'withered old ankle-biting hemorrhoid from hell,' eh...? How *dare* thee! Take *that,* thou disgusting spoilt little two-bit spinster!" The openhanded slaps on the right and left cheek balls & roses of our heroine's crestfallen countenance were totally unexpected after all the smart skelpings she had thus far weathered on her backside. These facial slaps were completely out of left field and stung her more acutely than the lion's share of other castigations and indignities she had thus far withstood.

And then, as if out of nowhere, before our disgraced young demoiselle had even had a chance to emotionally process, much less digest, the gag-awful tidings that had just befallen her, as relayed to her by her snuffy old governess, she felt her exposed nether cheeks being ferociously smacked upon with a wooden paddle that, aside from having the bedread holes in it, also had her nomenclature engraved upon it in bright scarlet letters (signifying some form of communal ownership, she imagined) that flouresced (reputedly) during hours of darkness. This series of spankings were being administered, to Yvette's utter bafflement, by Prunelda's longtime friend and soulmate Helga Armstrong, the dean and president's wife. Our heroine's initial bafflement, however, slowly transmogrified into a flash of enlightenment when she surrealized that Helga's personal grievance against her, judging from the sheer ferocity of the britching she was being accorded at her stern and steadfast hands, had more to do with the fact of our subdebutante's having been caught on camera begging out loud for Helga's significant other to smack her hard and bone her up the ass, in despite of the fact of its having been merely an unrealized (or, until only recently, semi-unrealized) sexual fantasy of hers. (Of course, Yvette Cartier would never in a thousand years admit that she had absolutely reveled in the untold pleasure of being ruthlessly spanked on her exposed back-parts whilst reclining in submissive recumbency upon the authoritarian lap of Helga's tall, stern, devilishly handsome old husband.)

And now it can be pronounced, straight from the shoulder, that our befuddled young demigoddess had been afforded an ample opportunity to experience first-hand, and to qualifiedly assimilate therefrom, that the sensation of being stung by a swarm of angry hornets was no exaggeration, such was the insufferable smart of each smack she had thus far gainstood. She might even be inclined to one-up that description by portraying it as having been akin to the stings of a *thousand* swarms of turbocharged *murder* hornets on *steroids.* The At-Your-Beck Felicity Conveyor permitted our crestfallen coquette to scree-out hard this time without its built-in algorithms deciding on the spur of the instant to ball-gag her, as they had earlier in the pledge drive. She figured that the machine somehow or other intuited (if that's the right word for it) that her screams of anguish would bring joy and pleasure to the members of the audience assembled about her, including the children who were accompanying their parents to watch her painful and humiliating ordeal unfold before their innocent young eyes.

After Helga had inflicted her stern corrections upon Yvette Cartier's seat of shame and turned the spotlight on blaming our groveled young prickteaser point blank for the fact that she—the wife and war secretary of the Dean & President of Pimpleton State Luniversity, no less—had just lost her administrative post at the school on miscount of every last penny of its funding in support thereof having been summarily withdrawn the day before by its wealthiest donors due to the luniversity's now plummeting reputation, thanks to Ms. Cartier's academic malfea-sances. After Helga had had her say and way with our impenitent malefactress, in despite of the fact that said war secretary to the dean & president was still huffing and fulminating with righteous fury, the Felicity Conveyor transported our dusted subdebutante to Mildred's Bakery, a shop within the store that was well-known for its buttery scones and fluffy croissants. Upon her arrival there, Yvette was deeply taken aback at the sight of her adoptive great uncle, the infamous war-profiteering oil tycoon, Harmon Ebenoid Weaser, standing tall and projecting authority on the floor of the shop in a baker's toque, barking orders to a floury brigade of meek and docile doughmakers, as well as to a self-important looking tabernacle of bootlicking pie & pastry chefs, all of whom were frantically mixing, kneading, and bulkproofing wet blobs of bread paste and who, judging from the manner in which they were collectively going the extra mile to ingratiate themselves to her Great Uncle Weaser by responding posthaste to each and every one of his whimsical commands (howsoever far-fetched or harebrained they might be), appeared withal to be his loyal & faithful stooges.

She had only met her great uncle three or four times at various family gatherings (mostly during holiday seasons) over the years, and the old man had always seemed to take a special liking to her. He had regularly bought her expensive & exotic gifts and was always insistent upon pinching her cheeks affectionately and dandling her on his knees like a toddler even though she was a blooming tween and, a few short years thereafter, a fully ripened nubile young sex goddess with a pair of gazongas to die for. She had never raised any objections to his treating her like a small child, especially as he had, from day one of her adoption, been her primary source of revenue via the seeming inexhaustible trust fund she received from him, in escalating increments, on the first day of every month. In despite of his being a relatively fit octogenarian, she figured he must have been on a triple dose of Viagra (or something of that nature), as she could never help but notice, to her utmost chagrin, that his manhood always hardened directly beneath her whenever she sat on his lap in one of her seductive lewd fashion micro miniskirts (with or without her diaphanous unmentionables, it didn't seem to make all that much of a difference). Although she had always been embarrassed by this "snake in the room," as it were, she felt that her Great Uncle Weaser had earned this special privilege of feigned affection from her, and besides, it was hardly any skin off her back.

Or so she had leastwise hithertowards presumed.

On this particular occasion, however, his unannounced visit was far worse than an unwelcome surprise. Indeed, the very last thing under the sun that our blushing young coquette would have had as her principal aim at this point in time was to be stumbled upon, stark-flap-naked as she was, with all the scarlet emblems of her disrepute glowing hot as a branding iron and shrieking shrill as a blaring siren, on the flush cheeks of her exposed posterior, by her Great Uncle Weaser, in such unpropitious about-standings. Instead of greeting her with the perennially lopsided expression of felicious lubricity she had long sithence learned to associate with the drooly old grinagog that constituted her great uncle in a nutshell (dirty old goat that he invariably was), this time it was the hard look of a stern, square-toed, Bible-thumping disciplinarian—a staunch Puritan on steroids, if thou wilt. The At-Your-Beck Felicity Conveyor ground once again to a screeching halt (the screech, of course, being a built-in feature, as are the distressed motifs in many manufactured items in accordance with the Japanese Wabi-Sabi aesthetic, namely: imperfections that function as marks of impermanence in acknowledgment of the transient nature of earthly possessions, amongst other things). Yvette was automatically hog-tied, in response to the Felicity Conveyor's built-in AI prompts, to a spit-like rod that enabled her to be rotated like a chicken in a rotisserie. Her Great Uncle Weaser, along with his subordinate dough-punchers and pie & pastry chefs, summarily pressed forward to knead her thighs, belly, breasts, and buttocks with their high-powered-exoskeleton disposable-nitrile-food-prep-gloved hands, as they would a bulk-proofed blob of bread dough prior to installing it into an oven to be baked. It brought to her memory the infamous German illustrated bedtime story in verse of the two mischief-making little snicklefritzes named Max und Moritz who, being inculpated for trying to steal pretzels from a baker, fell into a vat of the baker's dough, and were thereupon punished for their evil pranks by being baked inside an oven. Whilst her doddering old benefactor kneaded her nether cheeks and ninny-jugs with his calloused arthritic gropers, he expressed to her how disillusioned and heartbroken he had become upon learning fifth-hand that she had swindled and betrayed him by being caught cheating at school and stealing from her local grocer (who happened, hitherto unbeknownst to our heroine, to be a close friend of his since the days they had roomed together in college, in despite of the significant age differential between them). He informed her that he had no choice now but to tighten the faucet handle on her trust fund so that it would cease altogether to drip any more mint sauce in support of her dissolute life-style.

It was challenging for our plagued-out heroine to concentrate on the gist of the bad tidings her great uncle was imparting to her, as she was at the moment cogni-tively distracted by the provocative stimulation and exhilaration of being tantrically massaged on every avowed erogenous region of her voluptuous nude frame by the expert hands of nearmost half a baker's dozen of master bakers whilst being rotated on a mechanical rod in the manner of a chicken being spit-roasted in a rotisserie oven. When she felt like she was on the verge of coming, her Great Uncle Weaser—whom she had invariably referred to in her chronicle entries as "Weaser the Geezer" ("uh-oh...!" thought she, struck asudden with bloodcurdling dread as to what the revelation thereof on the part of her great uncle would portend for her imminent sweet by-and-by, whereto the repartee forthcame promptly)—started skelping and paddling her mercilessly on her needle-naked thighs and thunderbox whilst pump-ing up the volume of his voice to a screeching falsetto to pronunciate categorically his grave displeasure with her gross moral and intellectual shortcomings, never mind his heart-scalding anticipointment that she had failed so miserably to de-velop into the ultimate embodiment of unimpeachable maidenly perfection he had so assiduously bargained for in the hopes that she would be eligible one day to inherit his war-profiteering oil & arms contracting conglomerate. "Overmore," he said, "you have some nerve to scratch in your diary contemptuous nicknames for your most illustrious benefactor, thou ill-marred, derogatorious, shit-for-brains, aristobratic little cumbucket!" Thereupon he fervently pressed forward to spank her exposed buttocks dispiteously until which point the AI controlled sensors inside the operating system of the Felicity Conveyor decided on their own, based on collected psychophysical data, that our heroine had had quite enough of her great uncle's abusive smackings and defamatory vituperations (at least, for the time being), whereupon she was expeditiously disengaged from the rotisserie-style rod and conveyed into a closed compartment in the seafood section of the boutique that was permeated with a singularly offensive fishy odor.

Suddenly, as if out of the blue, a rectangular panel opened directly beneath our diminuated demigoddess, whilst she was having her ass cheeks and thighs pounded mechanically with a mock-meat tenderizing tool, and the visage of Werther Nemesinovich materialized, within spitting reach of our shame-faced heroine, as if he had been hiding all along inside a crawlspace directly beneath the conveyor belt awaiting his golden opportunity to gruel her and line her out. She noticed that he was wearing a blood-soaked patch over his left eye and was missing several of his front teeth, including an upper central incisor and first molar. The Felicity Conveyor, with its mind-blowing artificial intelligence, came to a jarring standstill in order to grant Werther (her "ex") sufficient time to have his say—and, presumably, his way—with her.

Yvette had never so much as even allowed this poor and poopy pathetic young fellow to lay so much as a finger upon her, much less peck her on the cheek or hold her hand when they had dated together in prep school, and yet now, for the very first time in his sad and sorry life, Werther Nemesinovich was confronted with the very real opportunity of not just taking a good long hard gander at the full measure of her magically seductive feminine charms but also of poking, prodding, pinching, spanking, goosing, and groping her, as well as leisurely fingering each and every hole of her defenseless young figure, spread-eagled as it now was (howsoever involuntarily) in the sight of his hungering headlight, in its all-encompassing nubile glory, after she had already been oiled, spanked, and diddled with a haphazard hodgepodge of pleasure toys and discipline tools in and out of every conceivable orifice of her voluptuous young physique by scores of random strangers, during which time the overall effect of the Lubricitrophin had intensified by a factor of ten (if not by a hundred) the insuppressible pelvic convulsions of untold carnal pleasure & pain she was presently abiding, as if sustained in a kind of Sisyphean state of suspended animation for the sheer sake of ensuring she would forever remain on the verge of a violent consummation without ever being able to effectively gain a solid purchase upon it. She imagined that Werther must have felt a complacent satisfaction at witnessing and, moreover, partaking of, this exquisite payback that was being meted out upon her exposed flesh in recompense for her having taken advantage of him to the point where he had been but a hair's breadth away from suiciding himself off a bridge tower, save for the noble intervention of his bosom friend Eiden, who had miraculously talked him out of it. Seeing Werther's love-wounded mug leisurely soaking in her private scenery from tit to toe was so unspeakably humiliating for Yvette that she could not help but weep hot tears of contrition and beg his merciful forgiveness (not verbally, of course, as she could barely speak, but symbolically) by means of the visual communication in her wide woebegone eyes, for having so ruthlessly forsaken him (in despite of her fundamental conviction, still nourished, that he was naught but a raggedy-assed beau-nasty).

Before she could so much as even offer him a peep of apology, however, he presented her, as if out of thin air, with a peculiar bouquet of neither red roses nor orange tulips nor pink carnations nor white peonies nor purple orchids nor yellow daffodils, but rather with something more akin to a posy of sympathy flowers bearing an uncanny resemblance to a potted aspidistra plant sprayed with bull thistle, knotweed, and quackgrass, the likes of which she figured one might offer (if one dared), in a more conventional setting, to pay one's condolences to a bereaved individual at a funeral service, whereupon he declared to her that he adored her passionately and would do anything for her—anything at all!—and also, in a seeming effort to ingratiate himself to her even further, expressed his vehement condemnation of, verging on righteous outrage at, the manner in which she was being disciplined for her transgressions by her redoubtable antagonists—never mind hundreds, if not thousands, of random strangers on the streets who (in his humble stupinion) had no legitimate boners of contention against her. She could read from his body language that he had meant every word he had said and that he was actually weeping sympathetically in response to witnessing her sorry plight. He surprised her then when he lifted his head out of the panel to kiss her gently on the lips as a kind of pledge that he would always be there for her. He even went so far as to give her his solemn assurances that he had currently in his possession a portmanteau of her personal effects that he had managed to pack up for her, which included a set of clean clothes he had looted from the curb outside her guardian's house right before the vagrants, gang members, and guttersnipes had had their go at ransacking through all the rest of her things.

Our plume-plucked femme fatale surrealized then and there that the eyepatch and missing front teeth were visible emblems that Werther Nemesinovich had fought heroically in her behalf for those precious lingering remnants of her bygone dignity. Whilst in the throes of her unreachable climax, she was overcome by a wave of emotion upon apprehending the unfathomable depth of Werther's love for her, and felt so deeply moved thereby, that she openly wept in his behalf, knowing full well that it was not within the compass of her moral and spiritual character to ever be able to requite a passion of such intensity, especially seeing that his comrade Eiden Dreadmiller was the man for whose amorous attentions she so wistfully longed. As if sensing her conflicted emotions, Werther gave her his scout's honor that he had salvaged at least one four-piece matching ensemble (with a Bergdorf Goodman tag appended to it, no less) that was awaiting her in the trunk of his Oldsmobile, which he had parked on the street just outside the main entrance to Mildred's Market, and that, as soon as the present cavalcade of disciplinary punitions and takedowns had run its full course, which it nodoubtedly would in good time, he would do everything in his power to see to it that, at very least, a superficial semblance of her erstwhile respectability would be thenceforth restored.

It was at that very moment that Yvette surrealized that she had been a consummate fool for brushing off such a tender, kindly, caring, loving, sensitive, not to say companionable, suitor for her affections as Werther Nemesinovich had affirmed himself to be, whereupon she wept to herself with unavailing remorse at how unfairly she had misjudged the poor man. She was less and less unfain to swallow her stomach and admit to herself in the end that her governess Prunelda had been absolutely right all along concerning Werther, namely: that he was, indeed, a nice young man and hence the perfect match for her. In the thick of her confusiasm, our poor little butterfly on a wheel closed her eyes and took a shot at imagining Werther Nemesinovich making passionate love to her. Which, to put it mildly, was no mean feat.

The Felicity Conveyor, sensing that their little kegmeg had been concluded for the nonce, buzzed to life once again and continued the diligently strategized operation of transporting our red-faced ingénue through its elaborate sequence of indignities, disciplinations, contumelies, tongue-bangings, and pasquinades at her expense. She was butt-whipped by children half her age; finger-fucked in her cack-pipe and pussyhole by a pomp of tenured professors thrice her age, and had her melons lovingly squeezed by an adjunct she recognized as one of her adoptive father's teaching assistants from the Dialectical Hermeneutics Department at Pimpleton State. Whilst being transported at a snail's pace through the produce section of the market, she had Asian pears, rutabagas, jackfruits, turnips, golden kiwis, sunchokes, kumquats, tiger nuts, nannyberries, fiddleheads, and a host of other exotic fruits and vegetables flung at her ninny-jugs, belly-nipple, and nick-in-the-notch from every which way by greengrocer wannabes who were violently angry at her for having been the contributory root source and cause of their not having yet received their long-overdue wage & salary increases in the past two-plus years of runaway inflation. They had drawn such seemingly preposterous conclusions through the instrumentality of a remarkable, if not unparalleled, feat of reverse-engineering on their part that permitted the emergence of a false premise that enabled the overwhelming preponderance of their blame to be shifted towards (and eventually embraced, and even nurtured, by the convenient underlying rationale that loosely connected their own personal failings in life to) our salt & peppered subdebutante's larcenous machinations at their place of employ. One of the staff members even went so far as to ram a lubed mutton-cumber up her love shaft and diddle her therewith for a spell of several minutes whilst manually contretacting her fanny flaps, which brought her to the brink of another powerfully triumphant consummation of her epithymy that she was unable to bring to successful fruition, just as a way of giving her a sound piece of his apoplectic rage.

The next round of corporal punitions caught our humbled heroine completely off guard when several sturdy yet slithery snake-like cables, which were fastened to moveable electrical pulleys attached to the ceiling, were automatically lowered towards her body and, through the agency of sophisticated artificial intelligence codes pre-programmed therein, managed to snugly secure our heroine's ploutsacks, queets, and forelegs in a series of complex knots from which she was unable to break loose, whereupon she was hoisted by her kickers towards a rotating turntable in the ceiling to which her tootsies were tethered and from which she was hung bottomside up with her feelers two stretches above the floor. She felt like a slaughtered carcass of a pine-root skinner hanging inside a commercial abattoir. Notwithstanding that she had been vouchsafed the free movement of her flappers, she felt appreciably more exposed and vulnerable in this ass-over-tit position than she had not a moment agone whilst buckled and strapped securely within the meat tenderizing unit and could now feel, more poignantly, the late November chill inside her backslit and touch-hole from the whistling north winds off the ocean, which only served to remind her of how univocally vulnerable she was.

To help turn the spotlight on the precariousness of Yvette's purportedly privileged social status, her ex-boss Celine and three renowned fashionista associates of hers from London, Paris, and Milan (including one ultra-distinguished celebrity Ms. Cartier had idolized from a tender young age) fired at her with their high-powered squirt guns whilst poking fun at the burning red marks of ignominy on her uncovered caboose as she squirmed and squealed in a vain effort to protectively cover her poop chute and love points.

The twelve members of the subcommittee who had initially intended on awarding our shame-faced prima dollarina a prestigious prize, in acknowledgment of the outstanding excellence of her academic scholarship, did a Jekyll to Hyde role reversal in their unanimous decision to act instead as a *snub*committee and resolved forthwith to raise cruent, angry, ugglesome welts on her unveiled derriere and genitalia with stout and flexile whips of all shapes and sizes, ranging from little snappers, fleck jump bats with wrist loops, and riding crops, to cats o' nine tails, cow-cods, and thunderclap bullwhips. At the very first stroke of one of these lathering utensils from the snubcommittee's strategic confectionery of correctional paraphernalia, our heroine knew beyond a doubt (from the word get-go, in fact) that these were not exactly what one would call "love taps."

Two of the twelve whippers from the snubcommittee were in wheelchairs and each was accompanied by a trio of care guardians. Be that as it may, in despite of their advanced ages and physical infirmities (one had a rare smiling disorder accompanied by other facial idiosyncrasies, and the other had a rat-sized tumor growing out of his nasal cavities that protruded from his nostrils and had to be held in place by a sliding tray connected to adjustable metal arms built into his special needs vehicle), they were able to handle their instruments of enlightenment with surprising strength and agility, hitting their target on the bull's eye with each and every rapid-fire stroke they executed.

"I want you to know," said one of the floggers to our disgraced young prickteaser (who, hanging upside down for the moment, was a far cry from being in what would generally be considered, by those in the know, as a position of advantage insofar as being able to make a fair determination as to whether or no the spectators in her audience were smiling at her in a show of support or scowling at her in a gaff of disgust) whilst adroitly administering painful beatings on her bare-skinned backside and front, "that I think it is important for you to apprehend, Mademoiselle, that, when we as a group, acting in our humble capacity as an appointed subcommittee, collectively decide (that is to say, by consensus) to award a prestigious prize in recognition of a given individual's allegedly outstanding accomplishments —whether scholarly, artistic, scientific, athletic, or humanitarian—'tis seldom if ever a matter that we as a body particularly relish, enjoy, or take lightly. Most of us, in fact, are deeply resentful at feeling burdened year after year by this unwritten obligation (which is only subtly hinted upon by the authorities under whose auspices we operate) to bestow such high-stakes awards upon parties who are most probably leagues more pampered and privileged and, in inverse proportion thereto, significantly less talented and accomplished than we ourselves are. And most of us assume this responsibility without receiving any compensation whatsoever therefor, in despite of our strenuous efforts to make the awardees feel at home through the generous hospitality that is afforded them in addition to the prize moneys they receive. And it's not something we do as hobbyists in our spare time either. 'Spare time?' thou sayest. Ha! The very concept of such a phenomenon is a sick and bloody joke! The lot of us who are assembled here this afternoon, acting in our capacity as a snub- (formerly sub-) committee, at the cordial invitation of our good friend Herr Dreadmiller, have lost months and months of sleep for the sake of attending tomorrow evening's ceremony in your behalf. I feel it incumbent upon me to bring to your explicit awareness that none of the individual members of our *snub*committee particularly enjoy getting up at ungodly hours in the middle of the night to catch flights that whisk us off, at dangerous speeds and excessively high altitudes, to strange locales two thousand plus miles across the country just for the purpose of bestowing this frivolously childish award on some perfidious ingrate. As I'm telling you this, you should know that my spouse of forty years is currently under hospice care. She was diagnosed with stage IV pancreatic cancer six months ago and is not expected to live more than a day or two longer. It goes without saying that she was quite pained when I divulged to her that I was under obligation to fly out here to award you this confounded prize. And she will very likely be resting on a cooling board in the mortuary when I return home. What this means is that she won't have me there to hold her hand in her final hours, something she had prepared her entire life to achieve (namely: to die with dignity and have her loved ones standing at her side), what with all her good works and whatnot. Is that too much to ask...? Tell me now, *is it...?* My only reason for being here at all is to lend you my moral support lest your feelings be hurt in my absence. Of course, all of these little niceties could easily be dispensed with through a Zoom conference or whatever, but we assumed you would prefer a more personal touch, which is the main reason all twelve of us flew out here earlier this week. And I am confident that I speak on behalf of all my colleagues on the *snub*committee."

Listening to this heavy guilt trip being laid out upon her whilst being mercilessly flogged made our chastened heroine feel incredibly horny such that the strokes and lashes of the heavy whips upon her naked flesh, as she hung upside down from the ceiling, only served to accentuate the feeling to the point where she could barely contain her luxury any longer.

Mercifully, the members of this venerable *snub*committee were sufficiently soft-hearted insofar as they evinced little by way of any seriously pronounced inclination as a group to lap their sacrificial victim any longer than deemed behooveful to intelligibly articulate their stance, as the intent, evidently, was to cause more psychological distress than bona fide physical harm. Thus, the fiery welts on her backside and front were mild enough that they would fully heal within a calendar or two.

After being trounced with this scutching for her shameless academic misconduct, our castigated heroine recalled a quotation from Edgar Watson Howe's Old Country Sayings that (quote) "a whipping never hurts so much as the thought that you are being whipped" (unquote), an aphorism wherewith she heartily concurred, now that she found herself on the receiving end of a by no means unrobust tantoozling.

CHAPTER FIFTEEN

B y the time the At-Your-Beck Felicity Conveyor had made its full run, and Yvette had been dumped into the discharge bin at the tail-end of the machine, she felt allutterly spent, and yet, contrary to expectations, *unspent*, as she hadn't yet achieved her ultimate thrill. When Mr. Justyce Dreadmiller advanced to the mics at the podium to deliver one final monopologue to his audience before officially announcing the festivities to be concluded, our heroine felt strangely let down.

"Ladies and Gentlemen," he announced, "I want to thank all of you for participating in this long awaited 25th anniversary celebration of Mildred's Market in conjunction with the unveiling of our spanking new 'At-Your-Beck Felicity Conveyor.' As all of you have seen demonstrated here this after, it is an amazingly versatile instrument—transmogrifiable, at the mere flick of a switch, into an upscale, high-ticket, multifaceted discipline horse, shame pole, and forking machine (amongst manifold other eye-popping appurtenances)—that I feel supremely confident will henceforward hugely enhance the pleasure and convenience of your shopping experience at Mildred's."

He paused for dramatic effect, and timed it accordingly so as to create just enough agonizing suspense amongst the more receptive members of his audience, whose rapt attention he now held, and whose insatiably morbid curiosity he had aroused by the lurid nature of his fundraising campaign, with the singular purpose of whetting their prurient appetites for whatever it was he intended to divulge to them.

"Now, gentlefolks," he continued in a softer, more intimate, nigh conspiratorial tone of voice to draw their concentrated attention to what he was about to impart their way, "I have some incredibly exciting news to relay to each and every one of you who supported our campaign this afternoon. Our initial fundraiser, as you know, was for ninety-thousand dollars for the sole purpose of raising moneys to compensate for what was lost from stolen inventory at the hands of this arrant little prickteaser here beside me."

Without warning, Mr. Dreadmiller slipped on a pair of sterile nitrile gloves and reached over leftward to frig Yvette Cartier's tight, depilated little vulva, as well as to tease her lovely nude, glistening little shame tongue with his thumb-ball and forefinger, knowing full well, from the abundant film footage he had seen of her multiple self-motivation marathons during which she had called out to him time and again for a hard & speedy deliverance from the ungovernable uterushes she felt within her seemingly unquashable crotchfires maint moonshines in advance of having actually learnt his family name, that he was doing her an immense favor by vouchsafing her the opportunity of fulfilling one of her most cherished humiliation fantasies, namely: being full body cavity strip-searched in public by none other than the proprietor & manager of Mildred's Market on the by no means unjustified suspicion that she had pilfered his pharmaceutical wares. He then pointed his right index at our heroine, who was lying in a heap in the discharge bin at the tail end of the Felicity Conveyor's belt, perspiring profusely, her face aflush, and her body convulsing in spasms of indescribable pleasure & pain.

"All of ye have had a chance to meet and greet our pouty little nymphet here this after, as well as to collectively communicate to her thy stern denunciations of her inglorious deeds by whatsoever ways and means ye saw fit, for which I heartily commend and congratulate each and everyone one of ye—righteous & upstanding pillars of the community ye have proven thyselves time and again to be!

"I think we can all concur here that there was no need whatsoever to involve the boy-toys in blue in this matter, as the punishments meted out by law enforcement agencies seld if ever suit the crimes in question. I like to see this as a win-win situation for everybody involved, including the offendant under scrutiny, since we have raised far more funding than we would ever have imagined possible. Yes indeed, Ladies and Gentleman, I am more than delighted to announce that—ahem, ahem!—as of the last count, we have hereby raised upwards of—drumroll, please!— Three. Million. Dollars ... *and counting!!!*"

Upon hearing these glad tidings, the audience inside the store, and outside on the streets, cheered and applauded the charismatic grocer with unrestrained enthusiasm. As the thundering ovation went on for almost fifteen minutes, Mr. Dreadmiller imagined himself as a world-renowned concert pianist on stage after performing a thrilling recital at Carnegie Hall. Once the applause had subsided, he cleared his throat and continued on with his quasi spur-of-the-moment monopologue.

"My treasured employees will now be able to receive substantially higher salaries and wages that will all but guarantee them more than ample room, inwith their freshly fattened budgets, to make down-payments on state-of-the-art new cribs that they will successively be able to call their own, as well as to raise righteous, well-balanced, upstanding, God-fearing nuclear family units that will prevail, for all intents and purposes, to prove over time to be providentially predestined to continue, for countless generations anon, and long thereafterwards, to champion the ethico-moral middle-class family values, morals, and principles that all of us in attendance here today hold so near and dear to our humble hearts, our noble minds, and our precious souls."

Mr. Dreadmiller diddled Yvette's vulva more vigorously with an eye to maintaining the peak of her plateau stage, which caused her pelvic region to convulse ever more violently. "Moreover," he continued, "my esteemed patrons will henceforth be able to enjoy all the fancy-schmancy, spinorty new amenities that will amplify by ten times tenfold the pleasure of shopping at our establishment now that our nifty new appliance has been properly installed and proven itself, beyond reproach, not only to be fully operational but also to be serviceable in ways that were never imagined in our wildest dreams. My good friends on the faculty of Pimpleton State have all expressed to me their heartfelt satisfaction that Justice with a capital J has been duly meted out to this fanciable young creature for her egregious academic dishonesty."

Mr. Dreadmiller clenched his fist and rummaged it deep inside Yvette's love hole to the point of driving her bonkers with unbridled lubricity. Being shy and reserved by nature, our raked subdebutante did everything in her power to avoid vociferating unseemly moans and groans of pleasure & pain, as she had no wish to be discourteous to Mr. Dreadmiller whilst he delivered his impassioned address, but, more than that, she didn't want any members of the audience to get wind of the fact that she was feeling all hot and bothered inside and was, at this particular junction, quite cliterally "dripping for it," as they say. By now she was seriously worried that Mr. Dreadmiller himself would get wise to how incredibly wet and clammy she'd come to be "down there," deep inside the hiddenmost grottoes of her tight-lipped little name-it-not. Justyce Dreadmiller, always the enterprising businessman, maintained his placid façade and continued on with his monopologue undeterred by Yvette's improprietous lack of self-control over the secretions of sexual fluids from the ducts of her expulsion mechanisms.

"All twelve members of the snubcommittee who flew into town last week for the purpose of bestowing upon Mademoiselle Cartier a prestigious award for her allegedly brilliant scholarly attainments, upon having been introduced, by yours truly, to the simon-pure scholar who composed all of her papers over the past several years, to wit: Dr. Dweebaldo Van Boofus, who is here with us today,"— Mr. Dreadmiller raised an eyebrow towards the audience as a signal for Dr. Van Boofus to stand up to be acknowledged, which he briefly did with a nod and a bow to members of the audience in acceptance of their applause—"felt they had literally won the lottery upon discovering a gentleman and scholar of such singular talents, rarified skills, and breathtaking accomplishments, and thence decided on the spot to recommend him for a tenured spot at one of the best known and most distinguished Ivy League schools on the planet. I'm also delighted to report, in his behalf, that he has been offered, as well, more than three dozen tenured professorships at other highly ranked institutions of learning, including Pimpleton State Luniversity and the Pimpleton Heights Academy of Art & Design right here in town. The dean and president of Pimpleton State, Professor Ulrich Armstrong, and his wife Helga, who were literally fretting themselves to fiddlestrings worrying that their school's reputation for academic excellence would be tarnished forever by Ms. Cartier's perfidious conduct, have been duly commended by their colleagues from a host of other higher education institutions, nationwide and abroad, for their expert handling of this problematic imbroglio. Mademoiselle Cartier's adoptive parents, both of whom are renowned academics at Pimpleton State, are delighted beyond measure to have found an acceptable excuse to kick their recalcitrant adoptive daughter out of their home for good and all, who (although they had never admitted it to themselves until now) had come to be something of a monkey on their backs—bloodsucking freeloader that she was (and still is, for that matter). They love her dearly, of course, but had come, in due season, to the ultimate conclusion that it would be in their adoptive daughter's best interest to get more serious about her studies, to say nothing of life in general."

Finally, Mr. Dreadmiller felt it incumbent upon himself to give credit where credit was due, so he asked Yvette, belly-bare-naked and welted all over her body as she now was, and whose glistening vulva he was still masterfully finkydiddling with his left fist, to take a stand beside him, which she had no choice but to do, albeit with instinctive reluctance. He then asked the quintet of dark-suited stern authoritative men to join him as well, along with some strapping young bucks from Yvette's college classes and any other sturdy young drool- & muscle-boys in the audience who wished to share the platform with our disgraced subdebutante. He wanted every soul in the congregated assemblage of bystanders before him to fully comprehend that, had it not been for this adroit young coquette's thievish subterfuges and fraudulent scholastic thick-spinnings, this fundraiser would never have been anything near the success it had enjoyed this afternoon. "And so," he added, "now that our nimble young femme-fatale has been softened up a bit, the hour has come upon us to light her fire one last time so that she can finally melt away and fade off into the sunset."

As soon as Justyce Dreadmiller withdrew his fist from our subdebutante's moist little cunny, she was jet-sprayed, as if on cue, with an ice-cold watery mist from the hosepipes and atomizers inside the Felicity Conveyor that were normally reserved for the produce section, whereupon she was expeditiously administered a purgative enema through the instrumentation of a rectal bulb syringe filled with milk, molasses, and a pinch of wasabi paste, whose lubricated tip insinuated itself mechanically, through the agency of AI coded prompts, into her rectal cavity for the purpose of expunging her of every last speck of her unspeakable filth.

One of the fundamental principles underpinning the design, development, and manufacture of the At-Your-Beck Felicity Conveyor is the perceived economic necessity (due in large part to global warming and climate change), by consensus of the designers and engineers employed by the Japanese company that had patented this singular invention, that it should be ideally a source of fascination not only to tech-savvy nerds and innovation-hungry futurists but also to technological dunces and dyed-in-the-wool Luddites, in short: to both those who are quick and those who are slack on the uptake in terms of how they choose to employ its omnifarious functions. Such flexibility and extensibility in its design and construction ensures that the Felicity Conveyor will continue over time to possess the inherent capacity for not just maintaining but also perpetuating its powerful mystique, lending to said appliance a universal appeal that is pre-calculated to extend from the lowest common denominator of the rank and filish to the highest uncommon denominator of the swank and stylish insofar as its attractive force to a loyal customer base is inherently predisposed, through the sheer force (namely: the "simplexity" versus "complicity") of its unique architectural structure, to propagate far and wide into the remote future.

And so, the beauty and ingenuity of the At-Your-Beck Felicity Conveyor's overall design is that, while it can accomplish all kinds of mundane tasks with near perfect accuracy at lickety-clip speeds, it also offers manual options for the technically challenged. In this sense it is not unlike a self-driving vehicle with analog alternatives for consumers who prefer to be under the vain delusion that they're in charge of a steering wheel, accelerator, breaks, and all the rest.

Upon having her bowels thoroughly expurgated, our humbled coquette was manually scrubbed down with rough rags and abrasive bars of soap from every quarter and washed thoroughly in all her bodily orifices until all members of the black-suited quintet of stern authoritative men had reached a consensus that she was squeaky clean beyond reproach. As the effects of the Lubricitrophin started to wear off a bit, our heroine could sense within her a progressively increased likelihood that she would lose control of herself if this gnashing tribulation went on for much longer. Several of the Felicity Conveyor's robotic manipulators, that were controlled by programmable electronic controllers, strapped and buckled our subdebutante belly-down to a kangaroo leather bed on the belt of the conveyor and then automatically spread her legs wide open and secured her ankles and wrists in fiberglass bracelets to minimize her movements so as to enable the quintet of dark-suited stern authoritative men to butter her bread on both sides, as it were, using high-end computerized AI coded vibrating dildos imported from Japan for the purpose of pleasuring her. The strapping young bucks from her college classes rubbed her from tit to toe with glistening love lubricants whilst other members of the audience, including Celine and her cabal of fashionistas, spanked, swatted, and slapped Yvette's exposed fanny vigorously and seductively. This time Ms. Cartier was unable to forestall the resolution of her climax any longer and finally found herself ambuscaded by forces outside her control which left her with no alternative whatsoever but to let herself go in such manner that she was propelled beyond the boundaries of her rigorous self-restraint towards a skyscraping pinnacle of rapturous ecstasy that could only be best described as "the Little Death to end all Little Deaths," which culminated in our hapless young demigoddess squirting a long clear gush of fluid from the very depths of her urethra, which, in despite of her state of hyper-alertness, caught her completely off guard, as if she had heretofore been comatose at the switch, for ne'er in all her life had she expected such an unspeakably appalling catastrophe to come down at such a moment. It was positively unhygienic and misbecame the image she had long harbored of the kind of individual she was, as she had hithertowards always managed to keep a tight rein over each and every one of her bodily functions and biological urges, including a fiercely despotic tyrannical control over her micturition reflexes. It felt to her as though she had just been waylaid everywhence from untold swarms of creepy-crawly scroncher-, eel-, doy-, skunk-, snake-, and nethercap-like critters that had been dwelling, unbeknownst to her, deep inside the murkiest recesses of her cloistered closet stool for God only knows how many years, such was the overwhelming shock this unforeseen eventuality possessed all distinctive earmarks of in connection with our discomposed subdebutante's iconic sense of her own uniquely autonomous personhood. And all of these agitated reflections revolved through her mind, spirit, and soul whilst the audience watched her with rapt attention as her tight little quaint squirted gallons upon gallons of odorless, colorless lady-juice all over the floor—in conjunction with ejaculate fluid from her overwrought Skene's glands (which were located immediately adjacent to her mystical G-spot)—near one of the buffet tables lined with drinks and hors d'oeuvres.

This drew heckles, catcalls, bronx cheers, hoots, and raspberries from the crowd assembled around her, not to mention eye rolls, dirty looks, and yawps of "ew, gross!" from the parties who were catering the event, and who, in a state of furious agitation, started wrapping up all of the untouched platters of appetizers and hors d'oeuvres into embroidered white linen table cloths to dispose of summarily for fear that the comestibles and libations they had spent all day and night preparing for this fundraiser had been contaminated by splatter from her aggressively audacious squirt, nodoubtedly out of overly conscientious health and sanitation concerns. Her squirting appeared to provoke a mixed reaction of sarcastic stupefied admiration in conjunction with scowls of contemptuous disgust, as the audience thereafter applauded our heroine with faux rapturous enthusiasm and at the same time booed her with unfeigned visceral revulsion.

With her daylights downcast and pearlings of lugubrious wiffle-woffles streaming down her rosy red chops into the eyes of her snorbs, this uncontainable squirting debacle constituted a veritable crowning of thorns at the ceremonial coronation of our heroine's public humiliation, each and every detail of which was being featured from all cogitable angles on televised simulcasts in over two-hundred countries and on all seven continents worldwide. These televised simulcasts were also made available for viewing by the astronauts and cosmonauts at the International Space Station, some 250 miles above the Earth's surface.

CHAPTER SIXTEEN

O nce this signally dramatic spectacle had been formally concluded, and the pledge campaign closed down, after more than five million dollars had been raised for the renovations, technical upgrades, and wage & salary increases for all the full- and part-time employees at Mildred's Market, and after everyone, including members of the staff, had left the store so that Mr. Dreadmiller could close shop for the night, our degraded subdebutante, who felt grievously mortified from having been publicly shamed in the worst conceivable fashion yet also breathlessly exhilarated from having just experienced the most mind-blowing imaginable moment of pure, unsullied heavenly bliss in the total entirety of her heretofore pedestrian day-to-day existence (in such manner, in fact, that it lit up her resplendently radiant complexion to a luminous refulgence as yet unseen and made her feel altogether at one with the unobservable multiverse), was escorted, blindfolded and handcuffed, with neither a penny nor stitch to her name, by a pair of callous security guards, through the front entrance of Mildred's Market, out onto the busy corner of Fifth & Main.

The handcuffs were unlocked from her wrists and the blindfold stripped from her eyes, whereupon the officer overseeing her discharge handed her the potted aspidistra plant that her "ex" had gifted her. Prior to allowing her to clear off, however, they made her sign a form acknowledging that she had retaken possession of all of her belongings (namely: the potted aspidistra). She felt singularly awkward standing there on the curb in naught but her lipstick and high heels holding on to this hardy symbol of middle-class prosperity. Our humbled young heroine could also feel the effects of the aphrodisiac Lubricitrophin kicking in once again, which didn't exactly help matters in terms of keeping her in a state of crystalline lucidity and/or acute hyper-vigilance to the subtle signs of danger that were looming all around her, nay, even besieging her on all sides. Our protagonist's primary concern at this point in time, apart from not knowing what to do with herself, never mind where to go, was the very real prospect that she could be arrested at any moment for indecent exposure should any of the passersby choose to report to the authorities what they would undoubtedly presume to be a show of premeditated attention-seeking mischief on her part. Such a scenario especially spooked her, as she had got wind of many frightening rumors (which may or may not have been urban myths, for all she knew) apropos of the especially brutal, intimidating, long-drawn-out interrogations and invasive personal inspections that were known to be conducted by stonily austere prison wardens and their teams of correctional officers in cases involving flagrant female exhibitionism, especially if the suspects under scrutiny happened to be young, nubile, and prepossessing, as our unfurthersome heroine most assuredly was. Such detainees were rumored, by reputable gossip mills, to be treated almost as harshly as terrorists and/or paedophiles, albeit with a faint patina of paternal tenderness deeply ingrained in the penile system to ensure that they remained, at bottom, blithe and content. Unlike their terrorist and paedophile counterparts, the young female exhibitionists were allotted well-balanced diets and afforded opportunities aplenty to stay healthy and fit with multiple hours of fresh air and exercise on a quotidian basis to ensure that their crimsony complexions would remain smooth and robust (for not inobvious reasons ...).

In any case, the welts, weals, and stripes all over our ingénude's raw flesh didn't exactly constitute the most favorable of testimonials concerning the integrity of her moral character. Random passersby glared at her with stern disapprobation, accompanied by face palmings, eye rollings, head waggings, and a host of audible tsk-tsks, tut-tuts, and harrumphs, all of which she found insufferably mortifying and demeaning. Amongst the familiar sounds of the city, she was able to pick out with her ears the faint howlings and screechings of distress signals and police sirens that were fast closing in on her from every quarter.

Be that as it may, only a minute or two after she had been dumped onto the curb with her potted aspidistra plant, garnering countless black looks and lascivi-ous gazes from a gathering crowd of pissed and horny spectators, and, moreover, feeling consummately unequipped to gain her bearings, much less to have any idea whatsoever as to how she could move on with her life, a badly bumped-up and dented, mud-colored 1967 Oldsmobile Cutlass Supreme pulled up to the fire hydrant next to the curb onto which she had just been discarded like a friendless stray dog. The police sirens from all sides were fast zeroing in on her latitude and longitude coordinates, which caused our hapless young heroine to work herself up into a tizzy out of mortal fear of being taken into penile custody. The battered old car's passenger window was rolled down manually and the passenger door kicked open violently from within by the vehicle's seemingly sole occupant, followed by the sound of a deep, penetrating, ever-so-slightly nasal, gravelly voice emanating from a dark uniformed figure in the driver's seat that ordered her to get into the passenger seat in a tone of voice that brooked no argument.

At this stage of the game our poor discombobulated demi-vierge had become so thoroughly conditioned by her totalitarian thrill sergeants (and hundreds of other self-appointed martinets) growling and barking strict orders at her from every-whence to the point that she had developed a kind of reflexive behavioral response of compliant submission thereto. She had, in fact, become so keenly acclimated to the foregone conclusion that she had no choice but to obtemperate with each and every one of the brusque commands that were being barked at her from every-one and their mother-in-laws, howsoever distasteful they might be, that she didn't even bother putting up any resistance to being abducted stark needle-naked at the edge of dusk on this gloomy late November afternoon in the heart of downtown Pimpleton Heights, for she found herself in sooth in a blind panic, with nary a place to go, having already been dumped out of her home by her guardians, kicked out of college by her school administrators, fired from her job at the love toy warehouse, disinherited of her great uncle's gravy train and oil & arms contracting conglomerate, and, last but not least, left in the lurch by the love of her life for another woman—a woman who, as it turned out, had played a pivotal role in our heroine's fall from grace.

Mademoiselle Yvette Cartier edged herself tharfishly into the passenger seat of the sinister looking Oldsmobile. Faded and greasy in spots, with an eclectic hodge-podge of ketchup, mustard, mayonnaise, and relish stains that called to mind the household-paint splashings of a Jackson Pollock canvass, the unsightly front riding seat was plastered here and there with strips of duct tape to prevent its passengers from being goosed by errant upholstery springs. She held on for dear life to her potted aspidistra, which she attempted to employ as a makeshift shield wherewith to protectively cover her naked sweets and pussy. Buckling herself in without even bothering to look directly at the creepy character who was abducting her in broad daylight, she sighed inwardly, resigned to her fate at his hands, for she had recognized immediately the nasal twang in his vox and had made out the blood-soaked eyepatch and missing front teeth from her peripheral vision, having already resigned herself to doing penance by giving this questionable young man her time of day... *again.*

"I love you, Yvette!" said Werther matter-of-factly. "I want to help you. I'll do anything for you! Anything at all! Just ask and it's yours!" He was accoutered in what appeared to be full military regalia, almost like a five-star general, what with a host of flexible metal epaulettes, service ribbons, badges, distinguished service crosses, meritorious service medals and whatnot. Upon closer inspection, however, Yvette surrealized that these decorations and awards were in fact forgeries and fakes, that they were in reality modified Christmas tree ornaments from Target, which made her wonder how well she really knew this man she used to go out with in prep school, and who had claimed for so many years to be head over heels in love with her. Why was he jumping through hoops to impress her with these counterfeit awards and decorations? she wondered. If he was really trying so hard to impress her, his over-exerted efforts to that end were bound to backfire upon him in due course. Or so she was therefrom not disinclined to infer.

Although he was beginning to sound like a broken record, our subdebutante decided to play along with his elaborate charade as long as was necessary before finding a suitable opportunity to abscond herself from his vile clutches. "I love you too, Werther!" she replied in a flat monotone, all too aware of her unabashed nudity. "Thanks for the ride."

After a few moments of cringeworthy silence, during which she could not help but observe, to her unpleasant surprise, that the Blue Nile diamond stud earrings from Tiffany's that Werther Nemesinovich had purchased as a gift for her some two and a half years ago, were now being sported by him, like trophies, on a fresh pierced pair of ear-flaps that were dripping with his claret. Withholding a gasp of disquiet, she welled up just enough courage to ask him timorously, "Um…, where's the four-piece ensemble from Bergdorf Goodman's you promised me…?"

"Here," he said, ignoring her question whilst steering the Oldsmobile away from the curb with his left palm towards the expressway on-ramp. "Let me put that plant on the backseat behind you, so you can sit more comfortably, but especially so I can afford myself ample opportunity to pay reverential homage to your stupendous appurtenances." He reached for the potted Aspidistra plant with his left hand, giving her a tight albeit affectionate little pinch on the fleshy part of her thigh as he did so (which caught her completely off guard) whilst only half-eyeing the steep winding circular on-ramp he was speeding on towards the crowded eighty-mile-per-hour expressway. Once again our heroine found herself clutching the panic bar on the passenger door whilst desperately reaching for the proverbial barf bag in the glove compartment, which made her wonder if Werther (insofar as his operational, tactical, and strategic driving skills went when managing speed and negotiating curves & intersections, et cetera) was in cahoots with her ex-boss Celine in a conspiracy to make Yvette Cartier's hair stand on end.

Aside from being unpleasantly jolted by Werther's daredevil driving (he was going seventy in a twenty-five-mile-an-hour zone) and dicey steering maneuvers, Yvette was at the same time shocked asudden to hear such blatantly lascivious innuendos being articulated with uncustomary flair, not to mention a certain cockiness of attitude—call it *panache* if thou wilt—issuing from none other than the normally virtue-signaling mealy mouth of this utter crashing bore of a man she had always known and referred to sardonically in her (then) private journals as "Mr. Quadrilateral." The unsolicited pinch on her left buttock did nothing to assuage her growing suspicion that she didn't know this man quite as well as she had assumed.

She had initially sized up Werther Nemesinovich in the blink of an eye on her first encounter with him in her sophomore year in prep school and had long sithence believed unequivocally that she had had him wrapped around the claw of her pinkie and, furtherover, had had him all figured out from head to foot, like the wind-up mechanical robot doll he nodoubtedly was and still is (or so she had heretofore reckoned …).

On hearing him speak to her so forthrightly in such slickly worded double entendres and, moreover, in such a sly and aggressively dominant tone of voice, she sensed that something left-handed was afoot. She knew all too well that she was in no position at the moment to courteously ask her so-called "ex" to drop her off someplace or other (prezactly where she couldn't possibly fathom at the present juncture) until she was able to find a way to make herself passingly presentable (i.e., "decent" by the puritanical mores of Pimpleton Heights), for, so long as she was in the altogether but for rouged lips, multiple marks of disrepute on her Sunday face, and an ostentatious pair of extortionately priced high-heeled stilettos from Saks Fifth Avenue that made her look like a gay-in-the-groin organ-grinder, she had no choice for the nonce but to be at Werther's unbounded beck and call, feeling herself under coercion to follow his orders to a faultless tee and then some.

'Twas right then and there that a not unfamiliar musky masculine odor assailed her snuffers from directly behind her, a sweaty stench of armpit-like sweat comprised in part of powerful olfactory stimuli she recalled having smelt just a few short hours agone whilst still ensconced safely within the relatively gemütlich confines of her luxury digs—an odor laced with the androstadienone pheromones that aroused and stimulated her sense of inexpressible shamefastness in a mysteriously peculiar way that caused her to feel both impure and unclean but which nevertheless attracted her to its source with an intense, almost irresistible, magnetism that, in its turn, made her all too well aware of a telltale crimsony flush of self-consciousness that was surging through her veins unchecked. The nerves all over her body (a sixth animalian sense, if thou wilt) tingled from a subtle current of air caused by an ever-so faintly insidious predatorial movement directly behind her that indicated the presence of an imminent danger close at hand. Her pupils dilated upon hearing what sounded like the breath intake of a Russian oktavist at the nape of her neck.

"And I, too," said a basso profundo voice that filled and shook the car. She recognized it immediately as the voice of the lecherous locksmith she had encountered earlier that day against her will at Celine's behest, who was now, to our heroine's astonished stupefaction, seated directly behind her. This card-carrying member of the proletariat, with his calloused workman's hands, cargo pants, and logoed uniform shirt, had ogled her in a way that had given her exceedingly uncomfortable vibes when he'd entered her apartment so boldly without her express permission to do so. The way he had leered at her indiscreetly whilst changing the pins and springs inside the lock assembly of her front door had betrayed his boorish blue-collar roots. The man obviously had no class. How in the world, Yvette Cartier asked herself in stunned silence, had she failed, upon entering Werther's ancient old gas guzzler, to have taken note of the presence of the hulking, thickset, seven-foot frame possessed by this powerfully built, broad-shouldered, mesomorphic he-man from the other side of the tracks? She began to feel something stiff and protuberant jabbing at her backside from behind her seat and whatever it was seemed to be growing inch by inch every half minute or so. S'far as she could tell, 'twas neither a fist nor a foot nor an elbow, judging from the fact that the throbbing pressure brought down to bear upon her from behind felt to her less deliberate than it did involuntary, not unakin to Pinocchio's kanozzle growing longer and longer each & every time he told a lie. Blushing crimson with embarrassment, it was all she could do not to admit to herself that this unexpected scenario was making her feel hot and heavy in a way she had never experienced before.

Because the second wave of hornifying effects from the Lubricitrophin was beginning to kick in with a vengeance, Yvette felt prudently hesitant to relinquish her vise-like grip on the aspidistra plant lest her "ex" and his hulking partner-in-crime take note that the nipples on her breasts were beginning to beam, which she categorically didn't want either of them to get wind of. Furtherover, her breaths were quickening and her heart rate increasing beyond her ability to hide those facts any longer. Before she was able to get a handle on the situation, however, the locksmith, who was foaming at the dick (so to speak), reached over the passenger seat to relinquish the potted aspidistra from Yvette's lap in order to fully expose her sex and sweets for the pleasure of his buddy Werther, overpowering our hapless ingénude's resistance thereto by the sheer force of his masculous muscular strength and weight.

Werther Nemesinovich refrained from uttering a word in response to Yvette's innocent query about her fictitious Bergdorf-Goodman ensemble, especially in consideration of the fact that his earlier mention thereof had merely been a ruse for the purpose of persuading her to slide into the passenger seat of his vehicle without argument (a vehicle whose doors, by the way, could only be opened from the outside, not from the inside, unless, of course, one had access to a proper set of keys, which the locksmith and Werther most assuredly did but our pretty young ingénude did not). Instead, he smirked silently to himself, with a triumphant sense of vindictive glee, whilst his good ol' buddy the locksmith, who had managed to masterfully pick the lock of our enigmatic young nympho, tenderly cupped and caressed her harmonious love-bubbles from behind, working his way down past her baby button to her everlasting wound with his rough-skinned workman's hands in order to arouse her ardor just enough to distract her attention away from his cunning accomplice, lest she observe Werther Nemesinovich reaching stealthily, whilst changing lanes at over a hundred-and-twenty miles-an-hour on the expressway, for a pair of Smith & Wesson carbon steel transport restraints seated on the floorboard directly behind him.

Awknowledgements

A special thanks to my dear friends David Denniston, Jim Davidson, and Ernesto Ferreri for lending their sage and judicious opinions and advice on my AI-generated cover designs for this novel. None of them saw the final design I came up with prior to publication but all three of them can rest assured knowing that their feedback made an enormous difference to me insofar as determining the book cover's final outcome.

Also, a special awknowledgment to my wife Kaori for her long-suffering patience, tolerance, and forbearance in putting up with me and my hermitic lifestyle as a composer & writer.

Always being made profoundly aware that there are so many blessings in life for which to be thankful, I have composed this modest little piece titled *Gebet der Dankbarkeit* ("Prayer of Gratitude") for piano, which can be listened to at the following link: https://soundcloud.com/gary-noland/sets/gebet-der-dankbarkeit-for

. . .

For any readers interested in listening to more of my musical compositions, over twenty CD albums of my music can be heard for free on SoundCloud (with many more albums in the works) at the following link: https://soundcloud.com/gary-noland/albums

Readers interested in purchasing any of these CD albums, may do so at the following link: https://www.trepstar.com/purchase.asp?mode=all&idpub=89760

Six CDs of mine are also available for purchase from North Pacific Music at: http://www.northpacificmusic.com/#

Almost a thousand performances of my music can be found scattered across the Internet on all the major streaming platforms, including YouTube, Spotify, Amazon, Apple Music, TikTok, Pandora, and many others.

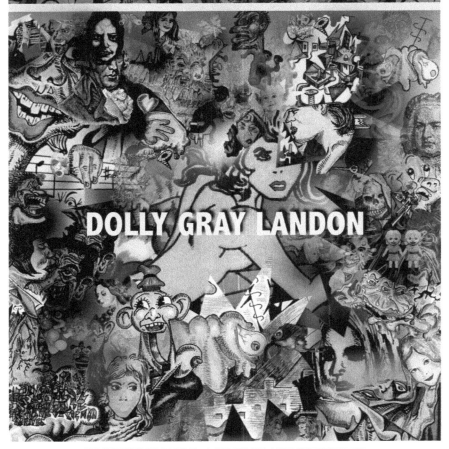

NOTHING IS MORE: A HIGH BLACK COMEDY IN
VERSE WITH MUSIC FOR SIX ACTORS. Available for
purchase from most major book retailers.

JAGDLIED: A CHAMBER NOVEL FOR NARRATOR,
MUSICIANS, PANTOMIMISTS, DANCERS & CULINARY
ARTISTS. Available for purchase from most major book
retailers.

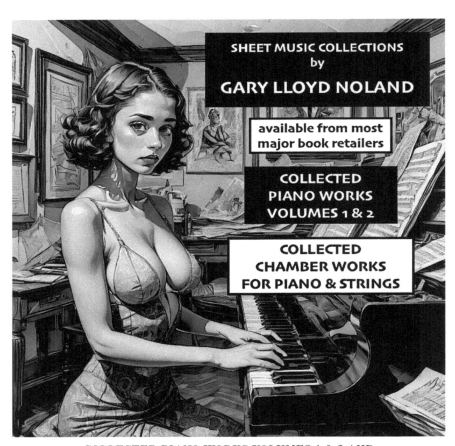

COLLECTED PIANO WORKS VOLUMES 1 & 2 AND
COLLECTED CHAMBER WORKS FOR PIANO &
STRINGS. Available for purchase from most major book
retailers.

**DOLLY GRAY LANDON (AKA
GARY LLOYD NOLAND)**

Acclaimed composer **Gary Lloyd Noland** (who goes by the nom de plume **Dolly Gray Landon** as a writer of plays and fiction) was born in Seattle in 1957 and grew up in Berkeley. As an adolescent, Noland lived for a time in Salzburg (Mozart's birthplace) and Garmisch-Partenkirchen (home of Richard Strauss), where he absorbed a host of musical influences. Having studied with a long roster of acclaimed composers and musicians, he earned his undergraduate degree in Music from UC Berkeley in 1979 and his graduate degrees in Music Composition from Harvard in 1989.

Noland's catalogue consists of hundreds of works, which include piano, vocal, chamber, orchestral, experimental, and electronic pieces, full-length plays in verse, "chamber novels," and graphically notated scores. His critically acclaimed, award-winning 77-hour long Gesamtkunstwerk, JAGDLIED: A CHAMBER NOVEL FOR NARRATOR, MUSICIANS, PANTOMIMIST, DANCERS & CULINARY ARTISTS (Op. 20), was listed as the Number One Book of 2018 by Amy's Bookshelf Reviews.

Gary resides with his wife Kaori in the Portland, Oregon metro area.

www.ingramcontent.com/pod-product-compliance
Lightning Source LLC
Jackson TN
JSHW062318161224
75546JS00009B/14